Denn

A Taste of Perfection

LAURA LANGSTON

Stoddart Kids

TORONTO • NEW YORK

Published in Canada in 2002 by
Stoddart Kids, a division of
Stoddart Publishing Co. Limited
895 Don Mills Road, 400-2 Park Centre, Toronto, Ontario M3C 1W3

Published in the United States in 2002 by
Stoddart Kids, a division of
Stoddart Publishing Co. Limited
PMB 128, 4500 Witmer Estates, Niagara Falls, New York 14305-1386

www.stoddartkids.com

To order Stoddart books please contact General Distribution Services
In Canada Tel. (416) 213-1919 Fax (416) 213-1917
Email cservice@genpub.com
In the United States Toll-free tel. 1-800-805-1083 Toll-free fax 1-800-481-6207
Email gdsinc@genpub.com

06 05 04 03 02 1 2 3 4 5

National Library of Canada Cataloguing in Publication Data

Langston, Laura
A taste of perfection

ISBN 0-7737-6274-4

I. Title.

PS8573.A5832T37 2002   jC813'.54   C2002-900839-5
PZ7.27Ta 2002

Cover and text design: Tannice Goddard
Cover illustration: Lorna Bennett

*We acknowledge for their financial support of our publishing program the
Government of Canada through the Book Publishing Industry Development
Program (BPIDP), the Canada Council, and the Ontario Arts Council.*

Printed and bound in Canada

*In memory of my grandmother who always believed,
and for Mom, who still does.*

1

Sometimes Erin Morris could taste things no one else could. And today she tasted bliss.

It fizzed and popped in her mouth, exploding into tastes like triple brownie sundae, double cheese pizza, and nacho buttered popcorn. Bliss was an "I'm-going-to-burst-if-I-don't-tell-someone" kind of flavor, and Erin couldn't wait to get home and share the news with her mother and father.

"Can you believe I was picked to work at the SPCA this summer?" Erin fingered the slip of pink paper she'd tucked between her books and glanced at Rachel. "Now my parents will have to get me a dog." The spring sun hit her square in the face as she walked home from Ridgeway Elementary School with her best friend.

Erin's face was stuck in smile mode. Even the pile of homework she carried didn't bother her. Even the second wart she'd discovered on the third knuckle of her left hand didn't bother her. Dogs and cats didn't worry about warts. Why should she? "The Society for the Prevention of Cruelty to Animals." She tested the words against her tongue. They sounded *wonderful*. "The SPCA."

"Um, hm." Rachel was clearly getting tired of the conversation.

"I know it's volunteer and three other kids were picked too, but this is my chance. My parents want me to be responsible and show I can handle animals. This is perfect!"

"Right." Rachel didn't even look at Erin. She was staring down Moody Avenue to Keith Road where three boys were rollerblading. "Too bad it doesn't pay," she said sympathetically.

Erin didn't care. She was happy to volunteer two afternoons a week at the North Vancouver facility. Thrilled, in fact. "When Mr. Parker called me down to the office along with those other kids, I couldn't figure out what I'd done." Erin knew she was babbling but she couldn't help it. Bliss was making her tongue crazy. "I couldn't believe it when he told me my essay had gotten me one of the four volunteer positions."

But her friend wasn't really listening. "Mmm, hmm." They turned the corner on to Keith Road where a gang of kids was gathering outside Winson's Market. "Look," Rachel said brightly, "there are the Oresti twins!" She smoothed her long blonde hair and began to walk faster. "Come on, hurry up."

Erin carefully tucked the pink slip back between her books and automatically slipped her left hand into the pocket of her jeans.

"Aren't they the cutest?" Rachel giggled nervously as the two girls walked through the crowd, past pots of bright red flowers and buckets of yellow daffodils, to the Oresti twins.

Cute wasn't the word Erin would use to describe Anthony and Joseph Oresti. Especially not with their mouths full of barbecue potato chips. They looked like overstuffed teddy bears dressed in blue jeans and gray T-shirts. Erin giggled. Even their dog, Patches, had traces of brown barbecue powder around his white muzzle.

"Hi, guys!" Rachel stopped. "What math pages are we supposed to do, anyway?"

Erin rolled her eyes. Rachel just wanted a reason to talk to the twins. Her best friend had discovered boys last year and every few months she had a crush on someone new. For a while Rachel had even been crazy about Erin's neighbor, Bruce, whom Erin had known all her life and thought of more as an older brother than a friend.

Joseph Oresti pulled out his math book and Rachel leaned close. Erin sighed to herself. Boys were okay — if they had something interesting to say and if she didn't have to look down at them. But most of the ones she knew mumbled a lot and were almost a head shorter than she was. Not only that, most of them were dumb enough to fall for that line about homework. Erin bent

3

down to give Patches a scratch on his head.

Poor Patches. The dog smelled bad *and* he was ugly. His brown coat was falling out in chunks, leaving patches of red, blistered skin. Erin didn't know if that's why he was called Patches or if it was because the dog wore a red patch over his left eye. Apparently he'd lost an eye years ago in a fight with a raccoon.

Rachel laughed at something Anthony said, and the two boys began play punching each other. Erin gave Patches one final scratch behind the ear and stood up. "Come on, Rachel," Erin urged impatiently. "Let's go."

"Hey!" A shrill whistle broke out behind them. The fizz in Erin's mouth dissolved. Her stomach sank. She knew that voice. "The crowd's all here. Let's party!" The other kids stopped talking. Joseph and Anthony stopped punching each other and looked warily at the newcomer. Slowly Erin and Rachel turned.

Deryk Latham. In a black leather jacket and faded black jeans. Sitting on his mountain bike. "Hey, Beauty." His washed-out blue eyes lingered on Rachel before they flicked to Erin. "Hey, Beast." He grinned.

Laughter rippled through the crowd. Erin's face flamed. Beauty and the Beast. That's what they were calling her and Rachel this year. And Deryk Latham had started it.

Erin looked down at Rachel. Her straight blonde hair never frizzed. Her skin was clear and her teeth were straight. Her jeans were perfectly faded; her white T-shirt spotlessly clean. Everything about Rachel was perfect. Sometimes Erin secretly wished her friend would get a really big pimple on the end of her nose.

Then she'd feel guilty for thinking that way.

"Don't be such a creep, Latham," Rachel stood up for Erin like she always did.

Deryk Latham turned to the Oresti twins. "And then there's Pork and Chop," he drawled. "With their dog, Stink."

The ripples of laughter turned into hoots and hollers. "Pork and Chop and their dog, Stink," jeered a skinny boy with red hair. The crowd began to chant. "Stink, Stink, and their dog, Stink."

Erin watched Joseph's face turn pink. "Come on," he said to Anthony, "let's go!" He grabbed Patches's collar and pulled. Patches dug in his heels and refused to move. The crowd hooted again. "Go, Stink, go," another boy taunted.

Deryk Latham smirked. Beside her Rachel giggled. "Patches really is ugly," she whispered loudly.

Erin fumed as she watched Joseph tug on the dog. Dogs probably didn't get embarrassed. Not like she did when the kids teased her about being too tall, or tripping over her feet, or all the other things they teased her about. But Patches didn't deserve to be dragged around — even if he was ugly. "Don't be mean to him," Erin said loudly.

"Sure, Beast, sure!" Deryk Latham lifted the front wheel of his bike and spun it forward.

The movement captivated Patches, who broke free from Joseph and waddled over to the bike.

"Go, Stink, go!" the boy with the red hair chanted again.

And the dog did.

Patches lifted his leg and peed all over Deryk Latham's back tire. He stood for a minute and stared at Deryk before waddling back to the Oresti twins.

The crowd howled with laughter. Even Erin laughed. That was one way to stand up for yourself!

"Hey, you filthy, stinkin' dog," Deryk Latham snarled. His blue eyes darkened as he stared at Patches.

"A first-class Stink job," someone yelled.

"Go, Stink, go!" someone added.

"Come on." Anthony looked nervously at Deryk Latham. "We'd better get out of here."

"Clear out, clear out!" Mr. Flores walked out of Winson's Market and stood under the red and blue Lotto 649 sign. His arms were loaded with the magazines he'd been shelving. "You buy your food and you leave." His black eyebrows were drawn angrily across his forehead. "No loitering or I'll call the police."

Deryk Latham left first. With another angry glance at the Oresti twins and Patches, he flipped on his helmet and pushed off.

Erin and Rachel began to walk in the opposite direction. "Latham is such a creep saying all those things about you and the twins," Rachel said sympathetically.

"He's a creep, period." Erin hated being teased but at least she had loyal friends like Rachel who didn't care if she was tall or clumsy. "Patches sure showed Deryk Latham," she said with a giggle.

Rachel wrinkled her nose and grinned. "I'll bet he spends two hours washing that bike!" She glanced back to the Oresti twins, who were following slowly behind. "I don't know why you want to work with dogs all summer. Camp's going to be way cooler . . . and you'll have to miss it." Rachel lowered her voice. "At least the twins will be there. I just hope they don't bring that stinky Patches."

"People shouldn't be so mean to him," Erin repeated. If Patches were her dog, she'd bathe him and love him and keep him away from Deryk Latham.

Turning the corner onto her street, Erin could see her dad's car. They were over a block from home, but the bright yellow Mazda was hard to miss. "That's weird," she murmured with a frown. Erin couldn't remember the last time her dad had come home in the afternoon. Maybe a few days before Christmas. But never in mid-June.

"Weird, what's weird?" But Rachel didn't wait for Erin's answer. Instead she tossed her head over her shoulder and giggled as she caught one last glimpse of the Oresti twins before they continued to pull Patches down the road.

Rachel sighed and turned back to Erin. "I think Anthony is cuter than Joseph, don't you?" When Erin didn't answer, Rachel continued. "What's weird?"

"Dad's home," Erin replied. "Early." A dog barked in the distance and Erin remembered the pink slip of paper she'd tucked between her two books. The fizz was back in her mouth. She couldn't *wait* to get home and tell her dad the good news.

"Are you sure you can't come to camp *and* work at the SPCA?" Rachel asked.

"No way!" Erin shook her head and began to walk faster. "I said I'd be available for the whole summer and I'm going to be." If her parents agreed. Of course they would. They wanted her to learn responsibility, didn't they?

"I wouldn't want to spend two afternoons a week with a bunch of smelly dogs."

But Erin wasn't listening. Her mother's blue station wagon was in the driveway, too. Weird. Her mother was teaching today. She'd left before Erin had finished breakfast. What was going on?

Suddenly Erin knew.

Her parents were cooking up a wonderful surprise. Twice that Erin could remember her parents had whisked her away on a mini holiday. Once, they'd gone to see a rodeo. Another time they'd traveled to Washington State to see the tulip festival. Erin's imagination kicked into overdrive. Maybe it was a bigger surprise this time. Like leaving tonight for a week in Disneyland. Her parents had been promising that for years.

Well, she had a surprise of her own.

Rachel stopped in front of Erin's house and gestured to the yellow Mazda. "That's still the coolest car I've ever seen."

"Dad says it takes corners perfectly. I don't know about that but it sure goes on the highway." Erin glanced at the house. The front curtains were closed. Maybe they'd bought a new TV — one of those huge thirty-two-inch televisions!

"They finally finished painting, huh?" Rachel's eyes were glued to the next-door neighbor's house and Bruce's bedroom window.

Erin nodded and tried hard not to smile. In spite of her crush on the Oresti twins, Rachel still liked Bruce.

"It looks good." Rachel pretended to look at the new paint on the house but Erin knew she was still looking for the basketball star, who was two years ahead of them in school.

"I've gotta go," Erin said.

Rachel pulled her eyes from Bruce's bedroom window. "And tell them your news, right?"

Erin nodded. "See you tomorrow, Rachel."

Erin's steps slowed as she reached the front door. She wanted to stretch out the excitement, like she stretched out the presents at Christmas.

Murmured voices came from the kitchen as she closed the front door. Quickly she poked her head into the living room. No new TV. No travel brochures on the coffee table. She pulled the pink slip from her math book and waved it in the air as she walked into the kitchen.

"Hi." She dumped her books on the counter and gave her parents a grin. "You'll never believe what happened to me today!"

There were no answering smiles, no encouraging words. Just two pairs of eyes staring at her. And the smell of stale coffee hanging in the air. She scanned the kitchen table. It was littered with papers and envelopes and a few bills. No plane tickets. At least none she could see. She glanced from her mother to her father. "You'll never believe it!" she repeated, her grin slipping just a little.

There was silence. Silence and a strange, flat look

in her father's brown eyes. Sadness. Erin couldn't remember the last time her father had been sad. He was always joking, laughing. She glanced at her mother but couldn't see her eyes. Mom was staring into her coffee cup.

"What's wrong?"

Her father's lips tightened.

Something was wrong. "What is it?" Erin asked again.

"Sit down." Dad reached for a chair and pulled it out. "We have something to tell you."

Her legs folded like two limp strands of spaghetti. She sat. Slowly her mother raised her head. Her blue eyes were rimmed in red. She'd been crying. Erin's stomach lurched. Something was different all right. Something bad.

"Is it . . . is it . . .?" She tried to whisper around the lump in her throat but the words got stuck. "Is it Grandma?"

"Grandma's fine, sweetheart." Mom reached out and tucked a loose strand of Erin's hair behind her ear. She attempted a smile but it only reached half her mouth. "Your dad's lost his job, Erin. He's been forced to take early retirement."

"Retirement?" She frowned. "That's for —"

"Old people?" Her father interrupted gently. His face wrinkled into a sad grin and his eyes lost some of their strange flatness. "I'm fifty-one, Erin. Not so young anymore."

Her father wasn't old. Old people didn't jog or cycle around the Gulf Islands. Old people didn't shoot baskets and drive cool yellow cars. "You're not old," she told him hotly. "You're the perfect age." She looked at her mother, sure she would agree, but her mother was silent. "Besides, you've been an accountant with Landers and Berg practically forever. They can't make you retire. They can't *make* you do anything," she said fiercely. "People have free will. You're always telling me that."

Her father nodded. "You're right, they can't make me do anything. But the company is in trouble." He tapped his fingers on the table. "They've given me two choices. Take early retirement or be laid off. Maybe even fired."

"Fired?" Her heart began to pound. "But that's illegal. We learned about that in Social Studies. They can't fire you without . . . without . . ."

"Cause," her mother said softly. "They can't fire your father without cause." Mom smiled and this time it worked. It was one of those 'brave' smiles, the kind she reserved for trips to the dentist.

"Right," Erin whispered. There was a pit of gloom in her stomach. She wanted to tell her parents about the job at the SPCA, but it wouldn't be the same. Not now. "Without cause," she repeated.

"They have cause," Dad explained. "They're in financial trouble. If they don't let fifteen people go, they'll have to shut the doors completely."

"We'll manage." Mom pushed her coffee away and turned in her seat to face Erin. "We'll tighten up, watch the spending. I'm going to teach summer school. Your father will look for another job. There's no law against that." She hesitated. "But I'm afraid we'll have to cancel your summer camp with Rachel. Maybe even see if we can get the deposit back."

"Okay." Erin nodded slowly. Her father out of work? It seemed so weird. "I have good news," she finally offered shyly.

"Right!" her father said with forced cheerfulness. "You said something happened today."

In spite of the gloom in her stomach, she grinned. "I'm going to be volunteering at the SPCA two afternoons a week this summer." The words tumbled out so fast her parents had no time to speak, no time to congratulate her. "You know how you've always told me to prove I could be responsible for a dog, well, I did. I mean I will! I entered this contest and four winners were picked. I was one of them," she said proudly. "So I don't care about summer camp because I won't have time to go."

Her parents exchanged looks.

"I know it's not a paying job or anything," Erin rushed on, "but Mr. Richards said if you're good and you volunteer long enough, sometimes you get hired on. And once you prove yourself, they'll even let you adopt a stray!" She waved the pink slip in the air. "All you have to do is sign this consent form and I'll be a full-fledged volunteer."

Her parents exchanged second looks. Mom's eyes filled with tears again.

"What?" The gloom was back. Swimming in her stomach like an angry shark. "What is it?"

"What your mother's trying to say is that this summer is not . . ." Her father stopped.

She could feel the gloom shark snapping at her happiness. "Not what?" she asked nervously.

"Not the summer for the SPCA," her mother said gently. "You're going to spend the summer at Grandma's place while we get things straightened out here at home."

2

Erin stretched her hand out the car window and let the wind rush through her fingers. The July sun was hot; the shoelace-shaped clouds trailing through the sky offered no relief. If her father hadn't sold the yellow Mazda they'd be traveling to Courtenay with the top off and the wind ripping the knots out of her hair. But the car was gone and everything had changed.

Everything!

Instead of working at the SPCA this summer, Erin was spending seven weeks with her grandmother in Courtenay. She loved her grandmother, and she loved the farm, especially since Grandma had started breeding black and yellow Labradors four years ago. Mom said staying at Grandma's would be like *living* at the

SPCA, but Mom was wrong. Sure, she could help out around the farm and play with Grandma's dogs, but she couldn't groom them or care for them. Grandma did that herself . . . or hired someone to do it. Working at the SPCA would have been her chance to show everybody just what she was capable of. It would have meant taking direction from other adults, dealing with the public, looking after sick animals. It would have meant *real* responsibility.

"I think parking gets worse in Nanaimo every month," Dad grumbled as he circled the block again and pulled up in front of the Nanaimo Bakery. Stopping at the bakery before hitting the highway for the one-hour drive to Courtenay was one of their summer rituals.

"How about running in and buying a dozen of those sticky buns Grandma likes, Erin?" Mom reached into her wallet and handed her a ten-dollar bill. "And buy yourself a Danish or something, okay? We'll circle the block a few times."

"Fine." Erin took the money, jumped out of the car, and slammed the door behind her. Her parents were trying so hard to be nice but she didn't care. She didn't even care that her father had phoned the SPCA and tried to fix things. There might be a volunteer spot for Erin in the fall, they'd said. But there were no guarantees.

There was a tiny stair at the edge of the doorway but Erin didn't see it. Her foot caught. She tripped. An older man eating a jelly doughnut gave her a sympathetic smile but Erin pretended not to notice. She'd be glad when her feet stopped growing.

The bakery was packed. Parents were buying loaves of bread and popular chocolate treats for toddlers in strollers. Business people in the small café were talking over coffee and brioche. Young people were stocking up on pizza bread and sausage rolls for an afternoon at the beach. Erin got in line behind three girls carrying backpacks and wearing bikini tops and cut-off jeans. One of the girls glanced at Erin before turning back to her friends. A tall blonde wearing black Vuarnet sunglasses, she reminded Erin slightly of Rachel.

The line was moving quickly. "Next," called a plump woman with a frazzled look on her face. Erin placed her order and waited. The woman returned with a bag and Erin reached for it.

The girl with the Vuarnet glasses reached for it, too. "I think that's mine."

"Oh, sorry." Erin backed off.

"Don't touch her hand, Sue," one of the other girls said as she played with a silver ring on her finger. "You might end up with warts, too."

Erin pretended not to hear but there was a hot, bitter taste in her mouth. The taste of anger. She watched the girl named Sue check her bag.

"I could live with the warts," whispered a third girl with a purple streak in her brown hair. "But if I had baboon legs like that, I'd die! Talk about majorly ugly."

Baboon legs? To drown out their whispers, Erin began counting the specialty chocolates displayed on a nearby tray. There were ten baseballs, six tennis rackets, thirteen cats, and six hedgehogs.

"Come on, guys." Satisfied that she had the right order, the girl named Sue turned to go. "She can't help it if she has hairy legs. Or warts. Any more than she can help being so tall."

Their laughter echoed in Erin's ears long after they left the bakery. Finally, after she had counted chocolates twice and was starting to count the bread, the clerk with the frazzled look returned. Erin accepted the order, grabbed her change, and bolted for the door, being extra careful to step over the stair.

Her parents weren't there. The three girls were.

Erin looked down the street and willed her parents to hurry up. She pretended not to notice the girls eyeing her. She pretended not to hear them.

"I started shaving my legs when I was ten," said the girl with the silver ring.

Where *were* they? Without the Mazda, her father was driving like an old man.

The girl with the purple streak in her hair giggled. "I used to think you got warts from touching frogs but warts are just a virus like a cold, only uglier."

"Too bad she has a couple of colds." They laughed.

Erin took a deep breath, turned her head, and stared at them. The girl named Sue looked embarrassed and elbowed the others. They quickly shut up. Erin decided Sue wasn't as pretty as Rachel after all. She also decided the girl with the silver ring had ugly knees and the one with the purple streak in her hair had a neck like a giraffe. That made her feel better.

When Erin saw the familiar station wagon and the welcoming faces of her mother and father, she jumped into the car and slammed the door behind her.

She handed her mother the change. "I got you and Dad Danishes, too." She resisted the urge to stick out her tongue at the three girls standing on the corner. Instead, she turned her back on them as her father pulled away from the curb.

Erin had planned to finish her Danish before she asked her mother the question but she couldn't wait. "Mom?"

"Mmm, hmm?" Her mother was taking slow bites out of her pastry. She always ate slowly when she really liked something.

"Can I shave my legs?"

Dad snorted. Mom looked at him and his snort turned into a weird-sounding cough.

"What brought that up again?"

"Just can I?"

"Like I said before, I don't think it's necessary." Her mother popped the last of the blueberry Danish into her mouth and reached for a tissue to clean her fingers. "You know I think natural is best."

"Natural is gross." Erin grumbled.

Her dad snorted again and Erin's mother frowned at him. "I don't shave my legs. There's no need for you to."

But nobody bugged her mother about it. Erin bit into the blueberry center of her Danish and then said, "You don't know what it's like." The words were muffled by the chunks of pastry in her mouth. "You're not me."

Her mother was silent.

"It's different for me. I *need* to shave my legs."

Her mother sighed. "You're too young to make that decision."

What did age have to do with it? "I'm twelve not three. Lots of girls shave their legs at my age. Dad?" Erin pleaded. "Mom's being unreasonable."

Her dad chuckled and stepped on the gas. Finally they were through the Nanaimo traffic and on the highway to Courtenay. "This is your mom's department, Erin. Not mine."

"Wait a few years," her mother encouraged.

"A few years?" Bits of Danish flew across the back seat. "I'll have a jungle on my legs by then."

"No, you won't." Mom grinned. "Like I said the other day, once you start you'll never be able to stop. And shaving makes the hair grow in fast and thick. I tried it once and that's what happened to me. Now I leave it alone."

Erin shoved the last of the Danish into her mouth. She'd never last a few years. She stared at the back of her mother's head. Her mother's *blonde* head. "But you're blonde. The hair on your legs doesn't show that much."

"That's true," Mom conceded. "But I still think you're too young to start shaving."

"And fourteen's too old." She wiped her fingers on her shorts. The warts on her left hand stared up at her. Her "crater claw," Deryk Latham called it.

"Hmm." Her mother rolled up the window and was silent for a few minutes. "Tell you what," she finally said. "When the hair under your arms begins to grow, you can shave that and the hair on your legs. See how you like it."

"Oh, good." She crossed her arms and glared at the back of her mother's head. "By then, it'll be so long I'll be able to braid it."

Her father hooted with laughter. Her mother gave him a dirty look. He stopped so suddenly it sounded like he was hiccupping. "And you could have hair under your arms by the end of this summer," Mom said in her "let's-be-reasonable-about-this" voice. "You just never know."

"At least let me take off the warts on my hand then?" Erin grumbled.

"We tried the sassafras oil, Erin. I don't want to take a chance with harsh chemicals."

"But they're ugly."

"Remember what the doctor said, they'll probably disappear eventually. If not, we'll talk to her next year about burning them off." Her "let's-be-reasonable" voice had turned into the "no nonsense" one.

Next year? She could be one giant, hairy wart by then. "I have no rights in this family at all." She slid down in her seat and stared out the window. "None!"

"What's all this about?" Mom turned and studied her. "First the hair on your legs and now the warts on your hand. What's the problem, Erin?"

Everything! Absolutely one hundred per cent everything. But her mother wouldn't understand. Erin continued to stare out the window.

Dad spoke up. "You're perfect, bug-face. Just the way you are."

"Perfectly ugly," Erin muttered. With a crater claw

and baboon legs and feet so big she tripped over them all the time.

"Erin, darling, we love you very much." Her mother's eyes were troubled as they studied her. "Warts and all." She gave her an encouraging smile before turning back to the front of the car.

The familiar phrase usually made Erin smile. Not today. She swallowed the lump in her throat and stared out the window. What would her mother say if she knew she'd tried to cut her warts off with that butter knife? She never should have asked about shaving her legs. She should have just done it. She'd just have to live in jeans for the rest of the summer. For the rest of her life!

The remainder of the trip was quiet. Erin tried to forget about those girls at the bakery and what they had said about her. Instead, she thought about the SPCA. Today would have been her afternoon to work. She would have done such a good job, too. And by September she would have had a dog. No problemo.

Now she had no dog and no job. Instead she had baboon legs and crater claws. Just what every girl needed.

Rachel was already at summer camp, probably giggling with the stupid Oresti twins. Erin could see it now.

The twins were standing by the lake, wearing bright orange bathing trunks. Their cheeks were stuffed with barbecue chips but they kept eating and eating. Faster and faster. Rachel stood beside them, in her new red bathing suit, staring up at them in perfect adoration. All of a sudden, the twins began punching each other. Bits of chomped and chewed barbecue chips began to fly. A huge wad landed in Rachel's hair. She screamed. Then a bee buzzed in for the kill.

"Erin, earth to Erin." Dad broke into her daydream. "We're almost there."

They drove through downtown Courtenay and turned left just before the Puntledge River. The city soon gave way to thickets of trees and rolling fields. A few minutes later Erin could see a large white sign with its bouquet of flowers painted between two stencilled horses. It said three kilometers to the Walker Farm. That's where Cassie lived. From there, it was just five minutes down the road to her grandmother's property.

"There's Cassie's sign." Mom pointed like she had every year since Erin was six. "You'll be glad to see Cassie again, won't you?"

"I'd rather be working at the SPCA and getting a dog than spending my whole entire summer in the middle of nowhere."

"That's enough," Dad warned.

Mom ignored her words. "I'll leave you some extra money so you and Grandma can go shopping," she said brightly.

Yuck. Her mother loved shopping. Erin didn't.

The road narrowed in front of them; the station wagon dipped down the hill and turned sharply at the familiar bend. Stretching as far as the eye could see were fields of green, dotted with the yellow and pink flowers of early summer. It was Cassie's place, the Walker farm. Cassie's dad was a horse breeder. Her mother grew dried flowers for market.

Across the field was the red barn and familiar gray farmhouse. Was Cassie there waiting for her? In spite of her unhappiness, she felt a rush of excitement. Cassie was her summertime friend. She wasn't like Rachel at all. She wasn't interested in boys or clothes. She hated shopping, too. She wouldn't care about Erin's warts or the hair on her legs. All Cassie cared about was horses. And practical jokes, of course.

Erin grinned, remembering last year and how they'd put raspberry Jell-O in the toes of Mrs. Walker's garden clogs. They had scattered a couple of earthworms on the outside of the shoes first, then watched from their hiding spot as Mrs. Walker had picked them off. They'd managed to contain their laughter when Cassie's mom had slipped her bare feet into the green clogs and let out a wild screech, and they had avoided punishment by offering to clean out the fridge and freezer. Even that had been planned. They got to eat the last bits of ice cream from four different cartons. Yes, Erin thought, she couldn't wait to see Cassie again.

"Grandma's dogs will look so different," her mother was saying from the front seat. "Remember that Christmas card? I'm sure they've grown. What was Grandma talking about on the phone the other day? About Blue and Duchess and a surprise?"

A quiver of excitement rippled through Erin when she remembered her grandmother's voice on the other end of the phone. Grandma had something cooked up.

"Frankly, I'm amazed she's stuck with this dog thing,"

Dad said dryly. "I figured she'd be onto something else by now!"

"Steve!" Mom shook her head but a small smile turned the corner of her lips. "I always said your mother would find her niche one day."

Erin had grown up hearing all about Grandma Morris's niche. A niche, she had discovered, was like finding a special thing to do. Her grandmother was always trying new things. She wasn't like Rachel's grandmother who knit socks and liked to cook. Grandma Morris was too busy to cook. For a while she'd taught yoga and then she'd gotten involved with a distance swimming club. She had been a tour bus operator and a home-decorating consultant, and she had worked in so many offices Erin had lost count. As far as Erin was concerned, dog breeding was the best niche of all.

When the station wagon slowed at the dented red mailbox and the familiar Dove Creek Kennels sign, Erin felt a rush of excitement. The whole summer was way too long but she still couldn't wait to see her grandmother. And Blue. And have some strawberry shortcake. Even if it did come from the store.

"Have to trim the holly again," her father said as the wagon made its way through the prickly green arch of bushes and up the gravel drive to the old stone house.

Her father said the same thing every year and every year she said the same thing back. "No, Dad, I like it bushy."

"Your grandmother and I don't." He tapped the brakes and brought the car to a stop.

Erin flicked her seat belt open and pulled on the car door. Even if he was out of a job, he was still the same old Dad, always wanting things to be perfect. She could understand that. She wanted things to be perfect, too.

"Darlin', you made it!" The voice came from somewhere off to the right but before Erin could open her mouth to answer, a large black ball of fur hurled itself at her chest and knocked her off her feet.

3

"Blue!" Erin gasped. A large pink tongue slobbered over her face and across her eyes. She wrapped her arms around the sturdy black neck and squeezed. He was bigger than last year. "Hello, Blue, my Lavender Blue." The dog shook with excitement. His tongue was frantically giving her a bath, traveling through her hair and around the back of her neck.

Erin tried to pull away but Blue wouldn't let her. "He remembers me." She giggled as Blue's tongue tickled the inside of her ear.

"O'course, he does!" Erin's grandmother hurried down the walk, a tall, smiling figure dressed in blue jeans and a vivid orange T-shirt. "Down, Blue. Down! That's enough, boy. Come here now." Firm hands pulled on the dog's collar and the Labrador retriever had no choice but to come away from Erin. "Are you all right, darlin'?" Peggy Morris pulled Erin to her feet.

"I'm fine, Grandma." Blue sat reluctantly beside his mistress, not taking his large eyes away from Erin and whimpering all the while.

"Well, look at you!" Grandma exclaimed with a smile. "You've grown taller." She gave Erin a hard hug with her one free arm.

"Too tall." She tucked her left hand into the pocket of her shorts and slouched forward slightly as she smiled into her grandmother's soft brown eyes.

"Not too tall at all, bug-face." Her father came up and gave her a gentle nudge. "No slouching now."

She stared at the ground. She was tired of her father calling her bug-face like he'd been doing forever. Blue whined again. His tail was wagging back and forth like a flag in the wind. He wanted to come back to her.

"Now, Steve, leave her be. She's perfect as she is." Grandma winked happily. Erin grinned.

"Peggy's right." Mom was always the last out of the car and today was no exception. "Besides, I slouched at her age and I grew out of it." She handed Grandma a parcel. "Hello, Peg. We brought you some of those sticky buns from the Nanaimo bakery."

"Wonderful!" Grandma released her grip on Blue and Erin watched the two women hug. Her mother was small and blonde. Dainty. Delicate. Petite. Like Rachel. All those things she wanted to be, but wasn't. She had her mother's large, blue eyes and everyone said she had very pretty hands (before her warts, of course), but mostly she took after her father and her grandmother. The Irish side of the family. Tall with pale skin and dark hair. Hair dark enough to get lost in, her grandmother always used to say. At least she said that back when she had dark hair. It had turned gray a few years ago and now Peggy dyed it. This year it was reddish brown. The color leaves turned in fall. That was it! She could dye the hair on her arms and legs. Blonde or maybe white.

"I bought your favorite dessert." Grandma wrapped an arm around Erin's shoulder. "Let's put away your things and then we can eat." They began to walk and as soon as they did, the black Lab ran in circles around them, constantly whining and jumping.

"You've got yourself a fan there, Erin." Her dad grinned at the dog's antics. Just then a robin flew across the grass. Blue forgot all about Erin and ran after the bird.

"He's outgrowing his playfulness some, but he's still a handful." Grandma stared after the dog, a proud look on her face. "Always chasing after something." She gave Erin's shoulders a squeeze and started walking again. "Good potential, but he's still high-spirited."

The hedge of lavender lining the driveway was in full bloom. Erin could smell the perfumed flowers as her legs brushed up against the skinny purple stalks. After realizing the bird was gone, Blue quickly rejoined them. He nudged Erin with the cold tip of his black nose. At the same time his wagging tail swished the bushes and sent a few tiny purple flecks into his fur. "Still love the lavender, don't you, Blue?" She brushed the lavender blossoms out of the dog's fur and gave him a quick hug around the neck. He answered by licking her cheek and staying by her side as they went up the porch into the house.

Erin would never forget that Sunday morning two years ago when her grandmother had taken the puppies out to the front lawn. Blue had wandered away and she had found him sniffing the lavender bushes. His soft black fur had been covered with tiny purple-blue blossoms. From that moment, he had been "Mr. Lavender Blue." Blue for short.

"Toss your suitcase in the bedroom," Grandma instructed from the small kitchen off the hallway, "and come to the table. Blue, you go to your blanket now. We're going to eat." Erin's mother and father were laying plates and gathering glassware.

"It's okay, Grandma. He can come with me." She reached out to rub Blue's head. She'd almost forgotten how soft his fur was.

"Just while you put your things away," her grandmother smiled. "But then Blue goes to his blanket while we eat. House rule."

Her grandmother didn't have many rules for people, but she had lots for her dogs. Last year, when Erin had come for a visit, Blue had been kenneled outside at night with the other animals. Erin had begged and pleaded to have him inside with her, just for the summer. Just for the summer had turned into forever and now Blue occupied a place of honor in her grandmother's house. But he still had to follow her rules.

Grandma had two of Erin's favorites for lunch:

grilled cheese sandwiches and store-bought straw-berry shortcake. Erin concentrated on the food while the adults discussed her father's job options. Blue stayed quietly on his blanket by the stove, his head down, his eyes studying the four of them. If only she could have a dog like Blue, Erin thought as she studied him. If only!

"His behavior is impeccable." Her father licked a spot of whipped cream from his fingers and nodded approvingly at Blue.

"I've been working on him," Grandma admitted with a slight smile. "He gets carried away sometimes, but he's the best dog I've ever produced. A real win-ner." Her smile deepened. "Meets the standard of per-fection for his breed to a T." She studied Blue for a minute before continuing. "He had that special some-thing when he was born, but I wasn't sure if he'd be show material. You know what I mean. Some dogs just have to grow into themselves."

"Like people," Mom added as she spooned up one last strawberry.

"Exactly!"

"How's the training going?" Dad asked.

"Very well. I spend twenty or thirty minutes a day with him." Her grandmother gathered up the dishes and piled them in the sink. "If I don't have time, John takes over. Blue is used to both of us."

John was a retired police officer who lived in Courtenay. He told great jokes and always carried a handful of toffees in his pocket. Dad called him "the significant other." Mom politely referred to him as Peggy's "friend." Erin wished everyone would just call him a boyfriend. Because that's what he was.

After filling the kettle and putting it on the stove, Grandma sat back down. "Now," she said, resting her elbows on the table and leaning forward. "I have a proposition for Erin." Her eyes gleamed.

Dad groaned. "Not another one!"

Erin giggled. Every summer her grandmother came up with propositions — things she could do to amuse herself while she visited. Once, Erin had stripped old furniture and sold it at the local flea market. Another year, she made tapered candlesticks out of the beeswax from Pederson's farm. Both times Erin had gone home with over $50. Excitement fluttered in her stomach. Earning money was one way to show responsibility. Especially if she managed to save it all and not spend it.

"Steven!" Grandma raised her eyebrows in a mock warning. "Hear me out."

"Do we have any choice?" Erin's father muttered good-naturedly. Mom gave him a playful slap on the knee.

"Something's come up with Duchess," Grandma began. "You remember Duchess?"

They all nodded. Duchess was Blue's sister. Peggy Morris had placed the yellow Lab with a family in Comox. "The Andersons decided to breed her, which was fine with me, providing they honored our contract and allowed me the pick of the litter. But just a week after the pregnancy took, Mrs. Anderson's mother became gravely ill. The family flew back to England to be with her."

Erin frowned. What did all of this have to do with her?

"I agreed to take Duchess," Grandma continued. "I'll look after her through the pregnancy and make sure the puppies get a good start. They're due in three weeks. Sometime around July 27."

Suddenly Erin understood. Her grandmother was going to give her one of Duchess's puppies! She hugged her knees to her chest and began to rock back and forth in anticipation. Finally, a dog of her own to love!

"What does this have to do with Erin?" Dad asked.

Grandma raised her eyebrows again. "I'm getting to that," she told him. "Just hear me out," she said again.

"All right." He held up his hand. "I'll wait."

Erin and her mother exchanged grins. Oil and water. That's what her mother called them. Her grandmother sometimes rambled, and her father was so impatient that when the two of them got together, they didn't always mix.

"I want to show Blue over the next few months," Grandma explained. "I took him into the ring last year and he did very well. He has the makings of a champion but he needs to accumulate points. I was going to do it but I'm going to be busy with Duchess and the puppies. I thought Erin could get used to working with Blue and take him into the ring for me. There are several shows this summer — one in Campbell River and a couple here in Courtenay. But the first one, which I really want him to enter, is being held in Comox on August 12. Then perhaps we can see about the other shows."

Disappointment licked at Erin's insides. Her smile slipped. She wasn't getting a puppy after all. And it didn't sound like she was going to make any money, either.

Mom sensed her disappointment and gave her an encouraging smile. "What an opportunity, Erin!"

She didn't say anything. She would have taken such good care of it. Her very own dog. Sleeping beside her bed. Going for walks around the neighborhood. Like she'd always wanted.

"It would be an opportunity for Erin, but it would also help me out," Grandma continued. "The more ribbons Blue takes, the better," she said bluntly. "I know Blue is a champion but the rest of the world doesn't. As a breeder, it would be a real feather in my cap to have certified champion stock." She smiled.

The show ring. Who cared about the show ring?

"A few dog shows would keep Erin out of trouble, that's for sure." Dad seemed amused.

Grandma frowned. "You don't understand, Steven. This is serious business. Erin would have to work very hard. She'd have to train with Blue every day. Get used to grooming him, handling him. Have him get used to taking orders from her. It's a great deal of responsibility."

Responsibility? Erin's ears perked up. Maybe she could tolerate the show ring after all.

"By the end of the summer, Erin would know plenty about dogs, and not just about Blue. Not only that, she'd be used to handling herself in front of hundreds of people. It's a tremendous responsibility," Grandma repeated.

It wasn't the job she wanted at the SPCA, but it was *something*. "You're always telling me I have to be more responsible if I want a pet," she reminded her parents.

Her mother nodded. Her father frowned. "Erin's a bit of a daydreamer," he pointed out. "I'm not sure she's—"

"Dad!" She'd lost out on the SPCA, she didn't want to miss out on this, too.

"Don't underestimate Erin," Grandma said. "She may be dreamy at times, but she's capable and hard-working."

Erin could feel excitement spreading through her like water through a hose. "That's right. I *am* hard-working. I like to daydream a *little*," she glared at her father, "but I work really hard. And if I had my own dog, I'd look after him really, really well." She couldn't resist adding that last bit.

"Mind you, Erin, Blue is far from perfect." Grandma bit the inside of her lip as she studied the animal. "He still surprises me sometimes. You'd have to learn to concentrate on him. Anticipate what he's going to do next."

"Erin can do that," Mom said. "Can't you, sweetheart?"

She nodded. "For sure! And I am tall for my age. It's not like I'd look like a little kid in the ring or anything." For once being too tall might be a good thing. As long as she didn't trip over her feet when she walked Blue in front of the judges.

Her grandmother turned to her. "We'll have to buy you some ring clothes, of course. A nice skirt or a dress. And loafers."

She gulped. She hadn't counted on wearing a skirt. Maybe she could get a long one to cover her legs. Or maybe Grandma would change her mind!

"Tell you what," Grandma continued. "After your parents leave, work with Blue and see how it goes. John and I will demonstrate what to do. If you catch on, and if Blue cooperates, then we'll let you do that first show."

She jumped up from her chair and threw her arms around her grandmother's neck. "You won't be disappointed, I promise you." She gave her a squeeze. "I'll work hard and concentrate. Blue is good. So good he'll probably take first place."

Her grandmother laughed and returned her hug. "Just do your best, darlin'. Just do your best."

But Erin wasn't listening anymore. She imagined she was in the show ring, with Blue. Wearing pants, of course!

Sound in the arena would still. All eyes would turn to her . . . and the glorious black Labrador beside her. There would be an announcement of course. "Introducing Erin Morris showing Mr. Lavender Blue. Bred by Peggy Morris of Dove Creek Kennels." She would move slowly but confidently. With Blue prancing elegantly beside her. Turning and stopping when he was supposed to, his head and tail held high and proud. Performing perfectly. Taking first place!

Erin smiled. So what if she had crater claws or baboon legs? Blue would be the perfect one. And she would be right beside him. Afterward, her grandmother's phone would ring and ring and ring. People would be begging her to walk their dogs, train their dogs. They'd pay her for it. Her picture would be in the paper and everyone would see it. The SPCA would give her the volunteer position back. Deryk Latham would stop calling her "Beast" and call her "Brains" instead. Even Rachel would be impressed.

It would be perfect. And after that, she'd get a dog of her own to love! Her parents wouldn't be able to say no.

4

Erin couldn't wait to see the dogs her grandmother had in the kennel run. While her parents cleaned up from lunch, her grandmother went for a quick kennel check and Erin eagerly went along to help.

"You'll see some changes this year." Grandma led her through the fruit orchard and the small vegetable garden to the building that housed the dogs. "John's been busy." Peggy's voice carried in the wind and the dogs in the kennel began barking when they heard her. "Okay, fellows," her grandmother called as she crossed the grass. "I'm comin'." She jangled her keys.

Erin smiled. Male or female, they were all fellows to her grandmother.

"I've got six dogs here right now. Two young dogs

from my last litter and three boarders. Including Duchess."

The kennel had been painted. Instead of its usual gray color, it was pale blue with navy trim. And there were new gates on each of the runs, as her grandmother called them. Even though they were long enough to run in, they were still cages to Erin. And though she knew her grandmother treated her animals very well, it still bothered her that the dogs were confined. If this were her kennel, she'd have all the animals in the house!

A full-sized yellow Labrador wagged her tail when her grandmother stopped outside run number one. "Hello, sweetheart." Grandma unlocked the door and smiled at Duchess. "Come on," she urged Erin inside the cage, then shut the door behind her. "You'll get a run later this afternoon, Duchess." She bent down and scratched the dog behind her ears. The Lab's pink tongue licked her grandmother's cheek in appreciation.

Around them, the other dogs howled for attention. The familiar noise made Erin smile. She might not be working at the SPCA this summer, but this was probably the next best thing. "She's so quiet." She gestured to Duchess who was a smaller, golden version of Blue, with a face just as pretty and eyes just as loving.

"Always has been." Grandma encouraged Duchess to lie on her blanket. Gently she began rubbing and pressing the Lab's stomach. "Dogs have their own personalities just like we do." Her grandmother was quiet as she concentrated.

"Can you feel the puppies?" she asked shyly.

Grandma shook her head and gave Duchess one last scratch behind the ears before she stood up. "Not enough to tell how large the litter will be. Maybe next week. Right now, I'm just looking for any unusual lumps or bumps."

"Hi, Duchess." Erin bent down and gave the docile Lab a hug. "How're you doing?" She was rewarded with a large, wet kiss that just missed her nose but traveled across her cheek to her ear. She laughed and wiped her face.

"Next is Butch." Her grandmother headed for run number two. The black Labrador was bouncing against the gate, his tail wagging fiercely behind him. "He's from the first litter I ever bred," she said proudly. "His owners bring him back every summer when they go south. He needs lots of exercise, this one. Okay, Butch, there's a good boy." Her grandmother pulled something from her pocket, stuck her hand through the cage, and gave the dog a Milk-Bone.

"I can exercise him," she offered eagerly.

Grandma shook her head. "His time is right before dinner." She walked toward her double run. "This is Pharaoh and his sister, Star." She unlocked the cage and went inside. "They're just five months old." The two Labrador puppies threw themselves at Peggy, whimpering and shaking and licking her face. One was yellow; the other was black. They looked just like Blue, only smaller.

"They're gorgeous," Erin said softly. She bent down and held out her hand. One of the puppies cautiously sniffed her fingers. That done, the dog decided Erin was perfectly acceptable and crawled into her lap, staring up at her with large, soulful eyes. The second dog waited for his Milk-Bone before bounding over to Erin and eagerly snarfling through her hair. A taste of cotton-candy happiness filled Erin's mouth. How she wished she could have a dog of her own to love! She pulled the two dogs close and buried her nose in their fur. They still had that fresh puppy smell.

A mournful howl pierced the kennel and Erin frowned. "What was that?" she asked her grandmother. It didn't sound at all like a Labrador. "That's Abby." Her grandmother gave Erin an apologetic smile. "John's daughter's dog. I agreed to take her while they went back to Saskatchewan for a family reunion. Come on," she urged. "You've never seen anything like Abby before."

She gave Pharaoh and Star one last hug and followed her grandmother to run number four. Abby was a two-year-old beagle who could jump almost as high as Erin's shoulders. She laughed out loud as the dog twisted and twirled in front of them, howling the whole time. "She looks just like Snoopy."

"She's a handful this one." Grandma stretched her hand through the cage and offered the dog a Milk-Bone. "If she'd been socialized better as a pup, she wouldn't bark so darned much. She's friendly, mind you, and very affectionate." She gave the dog's nose a scratch. "It's time for a run, isn't it, Abby?"

It was the chance Erin had been waiting for. The chance to show her grandmother that she'd be perfect in the ring with Blue. "Can I exercise her, Grandma? Please!"

"I don't know." Grandma hesitated. "She can be hard to handle, this one."

"Dogs always behave for me," she said confidently.

"Okay." Grandma took down the leash that hung on the cage. "Come on," she said with a smile.

But Abby didn't behave at all. The beagle was impossible! Erin tried and tried to get the animal to do just one thing on command, but the dog simply wouldn't cooperate. At first Abby ran in mad circles. Then she barked at the birds. When she got tired of that, she began a frantic sniff of the grass around the old oak tree. Finally she teased Erin with the Frisbee, running between her legs and barking at her from behind. It was funny at first, but with her parents and grandmother watching, Erin soon grew embarrassed. Maybe this dog showing wasn't going to be easy, after all.

"This one's not like Blue, that's for sure." Her grandmother snapped the leash on a panting Abby when the exercise period was over. "Once you learn a few basic handling techniques, it will come more easily," she reassured her.

"Look at it as good training for the SPCA, bug-face." Dad gave her an encouraging smile.

Erin chewed nervously on the inside of her lip. So much for doing a perfect job with Abby. At least Blue would be easier. She hoped!

* * * *

"Give me a call when you want to be picked up," Erin's mother said as she pulled up in front of Cassie's house the next morning. "Have fun."

Erin leaned over and gave her mother a quick kiss on the cheek. "Thanks for bringing me over, Mom."

"No problem," she said with a smile. "Say hi to Cassie's mom for me."

The old beige stairs needed paint just like they had last year — and the year before that. Some things never changed. Like the stairs. And Cassie.

Cassie opened the door before she could knock. Erin stared, shocked. Cassie, her summertime friend who had been the same for as long as she could remember, wasn't the same at all!

"It's me, silly!" Cassie grinned and pulled her inside. "What do you like more? My ear cuff or my hair?"

"I'm . . . I'm not sure!" She tried to grin back but her face was stuck. Cassie wasn't even wearing her usual jeans. This was weird. "They're both so . . . so . . . different!" She managed a weak smile.

Cassie spun around and her black jumper flared out from her legs. But this time her long red hair didn't fly out with her. It stayed short and neat against her head. "They cut it even shorter at the back. See?"

Her friend's hair was tapered to a neat V at her neck. "Wow, Cass, you always swore you'd never cut it." Cassie's long hair was as much a part of her as the horses she loved to ride and the Nancy Drew books she loved to read. "What happened?"

"Grade seven happened, silly. Junior high." Cassie

rolled her eyes. "It's way different than elementary school."

Of course. In Courtenay, elementary school ended in grade six. Not in North Vancouver. "I'll be at Ridgeway Elementary for another year, remember?"

"Right." Cassie nodded. "But you'll be the oldest in the school," she pointed out. "Kids will be looking up to you. In my case, the kids were looking down on me. They were dying their hair purple and ripping their jeans. I looked like a baby beside them. My mom had a fit when I told her I wanted to do that, but I had to do something. Be different. Treena said I needed to do a reinvention. It's kind of like a makeover." She shrugged again. "So I did."

Treena was Cassie's older sister. She was in grade ten. The glamor queen, Erin called her. "A reinvention, huh?"

"Since the other kids were wearing jeans, I decided I'd be different and wear skirts and dresses. Mom *loved* that idea. But when I tried wearing lipstick to school, she caught me and that was the end of that, you know? Then I complained about how they treated me like a baby and Dad went out and bought me an ear cuff like Treena's and then he and Mom had the hugest fight." Cassie giggled. "Mom was almost purple, she was so mad. But I got to keep it." She stopped talking suddenly and stared up at Erin. "Hey, when did you get so tall?"

She felt it again. That feeling she got when people stared at her. That feeling like she wanted to drop into a big black hole and never come out. "It just sort of happened." She could have told the old Cassie every-thing. But she wasn't sure about this new version.

"Come on." Cassie grabbed her arm and dragged her down the hall to her bedroom. "I got a new gold-fish named Mr. Phillips. You've got to see him."

Cassie's room was just as messy as usual. Her bed was piled with books, her dresser was piled with clothes, her riding gear tumbled out of the closet. Even the fat Mr. Phillips happily swam in a fish bowl that was crammed next to Cassie's radio, magazines, two dirty glasses, and a pile of Lip Smackers. Cassie pushed aside some books and the two girls settled on the bed.

"So," Cassie said, crossing her legs and leaning for-ward, "how is it being tall anyway?"

Erin smiled. In spite of Cassie's reinvention, her old friend *was* the same. Always ready to get right to the things that mattered. "Terrible," she confessed. "The boys all tease me and my feet are too big and I forget how tall I am and I sometimes bump into things. Not only that, look at this." She held out her left hand and showed Cassie her knuckle. "Warts. Mom used some natural sassafras oil but it didn't work and she says I have to wait and let them go away on their own."

"Yuck!" Cassie gave her a sympathetic smile. "I had warts on the bottom of my foot once. For a whole summer. At least you don't have to walk on them," she said.

Erin rolled up the hem of her jeans until half her leg was showing. "And look," she said.

Cassie looked down and back up again. "I've seen your legs before, Erin. What's the big deal?"

She wanted to tell Cassie about baboon legs and crater claw and how awful it felt when everyone laughed, but she couldn't get around the lump in her throat. "The hair," she whispered. "Look at it all."

Cassie looked. "So, you've got hair on your legs. So do I." She held out her leg for Erin to see. "What's the big deal?" she asked again.

Erin stared at the two legs side by side. One short and tanned, covered with pale peach fuzz. The other long and pale, thick with dark hair. "Your hair's light." She pointed to Cassie's leg. "Mine's dark. And I've got lots more of it than I did last year. That's the big deal."

Cassie tucked her leg away. "So shave your legs. Lots of girls do."

"I know," She sighed. "But Mom won't let me."

"Oh." Cassie was silent. She understood exactly. Her mother could be strict, too.

Suddenly Erin felt like she had to defend her parents. "It's been tough this last little while. My dad lost his job. He . . . he . . . was sort of forced to take early retirement. He's been busy looking for work and Mom's been kind of worried about him, so I haven't wanted to bug them much and . . . I don't know." She stopped. "Mom doesn't believe in shaving but she says when I grow hair under my arms maybe I can shave that and the hair on my legs."

Cassie snorted. "Great. Nothing like waiting around for the hair under your arms to grow." She flapped her arms like they were wings. "Hurry up, hair. Grow." She started to giggle. So did Erin. Pretty soon the two girls were rolling on the bed, holding their stomachs and howling with laughter.

After a minute, there was a loud bang on Cassie's bedroom door. "Must be Erin Morris in there," a cheerful voice yelled through the door. "Hi, Erin."

"Hi . . ." Erin gasped through bursts of laughter. "Hi, Treena." She could hear the older girl whistling as she went down the hall to her bedroom.

"It's not that bad, Erin," Cassie reassured her. "Lots of girls have hair on their legs. Just wear pants for a while. Till the hair under your arms grows in." She giggled again.

"Except I can't in the ring. At least Grandma doesn't want me to. She's talking about buying me a skirt."

Cassie leaned past the pile of magazines stacked near her fish and pulled out a small red box. "What ring?" She held out a bag full of broken peppermint pieces.

"The dog ring." Erin picked out the largest piece she could find. "Grandma says I can show Blue this summer. But she wants me to wear a skirt and loafers."

"Your grandma's cool." Cassie helped herself to a candy. "She'll understand if you want to wear pants."

The fresh taste of mint flowed through Erin's mouth. "Maybe." She took a deep breath and let the smell fill her nose. "But the look is important, you know. To impress the judges."

Cassie nodded and fell silent. She'd been to enough horse shows to know exactly what Erin was talking about. "Your parents are only here for a couple of days, right? And then they go back to Vancouver." Cassie knew the routine. Erin's parents always brought her on a Friday and left Sunday morning.

"They leave tomorrow." She didn't like the gleam in Cassie's eye. It was the same gleam she'd had last year when she decided they should raid the Wellspring Apple Orchard.

"So when they leave, we'll start." Cassie's candy clinked against her teeth. "We'll reinvent you just like Treena reinvented me." She cocked her head to the side and studied Erin's hair. "We'll start at the top and work down. We'll change your hair, we'll dump your warts, we'll fix your legs. We'll change lots and lots of things. It'll be a totally new you."

Erin stared at the totally new Cassie. What else did her friend have in mind? Knowing Cassie, lots. "I'm not sure I want a totally new me," she admitted. "I just want a better me. A perfect me."

Cassie leaned forward until her nose was almost touching Erin's. "Of course, you do. Treena will help." She jumped up, grabbed paper and a pen from the pile on her dresser, and flopped back down on the bed. "First we'll make a list. We don't want to miss anything. When is the dog show anyway?" Cassie's pen was poised over the paper.

"August 12th."

"Lots of time to plan," Cassie said, beginning to write. "Hair. Face. Warts." She looked up, studied Erin for a minute, and bent her head again. "Eyebrows. Nails. Treena gives great manicures," she said brightly. "Hair on legs." She glanced up, a sly grin on her face. "When I'm finished, your legs will be smoother than a Popsicle!"

In spite of her hesitation, Erin was catching Cassie's excitement. No warts, smooth legs. Nothing for the kids to tease her about. It would be perfect. *She* would be perfect. A perfect Erin Morris to go with Blue in the show ring.

"Leave it to me," Cassie said mysteriously. "Me and Treena. We'll give you the perfect reinvention this summer. You can wow the judges at the dog show and go home and wow the boys in grade seven."

She groaned out loud. Not Cassie too! "Since when did you get interested in boys?" she asked peevishly.

Cassie chuckled and looked up. "You just wait, Erin. Grade seven changes things. Lots and lots of things!"

5

The next morning, just a few minutes after her parents had packed up and left, Erin heard the crunch of car tires on the gravel outside.

"Woof!" Blue jumped up from his bed by the stove and went expectantly to the door.

She followed him. Maybe her parents had forgotten something. She opened the door to check and Blue raced out between her legs.

Her grandmother came up and looked over her shoulder. "It's John," Grandma said with a smile. Quickly she went down the steps to greet him. Erin followed.

Crouched beside the back wheel of his red Jeep, John Travers was tousling with Blue. "Long time no see, Missy." When he smiled at Erin, the skin around his blue eyes crinkled. "How's life over there in the big city?" He reached into the pocket of his jeans and pulled something out. "Catch." He tossed a small beige square into the air.

The caramel landed smack in the middle of her palm. She grinned. Same old John. "Life's fine." At least John hadn't said anything about her getting taller. She unwrapped the soft candy and put it in her mouth. Things *would* be fine. Two months in Courtenay wouldn't be so bad, especially when she had Blue to train with. And Cassie to hang out with.

John pulled a paper bag from the Jeep. "Brought you a present," he said.

Erin flushed with a mixture of pleasure and embarrassment. "Hey, thanks!"

"Actually it's a present for you and Blue," John explained as she reached into the bag.

Her fingers closed around something metallic. She pulled it out and frowned. She had no idea what it was! It looked like a big metal U with a coiled spring on one end. Puzzled, she looked up at John. Maybe it was some kind of joke.

Her grandmother beamed. "I never would have thought of it. What a great idea!"

"I thought so." John smiled back.

Erin looked back at the giant U she held in her hand. She turned it sideways. That way it looked more like a triangle. She frowned.

"Shall we tell her what it is?" her grandmother teased.

John chuckled. "Maybe we should make her guess."

"I give up," Erin told them. "What is it?"

"It's called a springer, m'darlin'. It's for bike riding with Blue."

"Oh." She looked at the metal U again. A springer. She couldn't see how it worked — or why she needed it.

John answered both of her questions. "See this end?" He pointed. "You attach this to your bike and then . . ." His fingers ran down the U and up the other end, "this end has the spring and attaches to Blue's harness. That way he can run beside your bike without getting caught in a leash. And he'll get the exercise he needs to get in shape for the show."

"Last year when I took Blue out, he just ran beside the bike," Erin said.

Grandma nodded. "I know, but traffic has picked up around here," she explained. "And Blue is so quick. It's probably a good idea to keep him on his harness when you're out riding."

"Sure." She bent down beside Blue to let him sniff the metal. "What do you think, Blue? You going to like running with the springer?"

The dog wagged his tail and rolled his tongue across Erin's face. She smiled. "He approves."

John reached out and gave Blue a quick pat on the head. "I thought he would." He turned to Erin. "I understand it's down to work today."

She nodded and sucked on the sweet caramel.

"Do I have time for a coffee first?" He raised his eyebrows in a silent question.

"Of course!" Grandma turned to Erin. "Why don't you take Blue into the yard and let him run off some steam? We'll be there soon."

The other dogs were howling and yapping in the kennel but she tried to ignore them as she tossed the Frisbee for Blue. It was hard! She wanted to go right over and let them all out. All except Abby! That dog was too much to handle.

"Go, Blue, go!" Delighted, the dog bounced back and forth, catching and retrieving. Even though it wasn't yet noon, the sun was high and hot in the summer sky. She lifted the hair on the back of her neck and wiped away the dampness. Maybe if she put it in a ponytail, she'd feel better. But she didn't have a fastener with her and she didn't feel like going back into the house. Instead Erin coiled her hair into a knot, tucked it into her shirt, and tossed the Frisbee again for Blue.

Fetch and toss. Fetch and toss. Back and forth Blue went. She grew hot just watching him run. She wiped her sweaty palms on her jeans and threw the Frisbee yet another time. If she'd worn shorts like Grandma had suggested, she wouldn't be feeling so hot and sticky right now. Never mind. If Blue could race around with all that fur on his body, she could wear jeans.

After a while, the heat got to Blue, too. By the time John and Grandma came back, he was lying at Erin's feet, his body panting with exertion.

"Here you go, boy. This'll cool you off." Grandma placed a bowl of water on the ground and Blue gratefully lapped it up. "John will walk you through the routine." She handed Erin a dog leash. "I'm going to clean the kennels. I'll check back with you two in a little while."

John reached into his pocket. Erin expected him to pull out another caramel. Instead he pulled out some dried dog treats. "Bait," he explained as he held the small brown square out to Blue. "You'll need to have bait in your pocket during training and in the ring. Sit, Blue," John ordered.

Blue sat.

"Okay." John nodded.

Gently the Lab took the treat John offered. His dark eyes remained glued on John's face.

"The first thing you'll want to do before you go into the ring is groom your dog." John reached out to stroke Blue's ears. "We'll go over that another day. And we'll spend some time on anatomy then, too. Today we'll spend about twenty minutes on the routine."

A rush of excitement swept through Erin, and it bubbled in her mouth like those tiny exploding candies she loved. She was actually going to take Blue into the show ring next month! She and Blue would be great together! She just *knew* they would be.

"We'll do gaiting first, and Blue will do that on lead. Take the leash and put it on Blue," John instructed.

Erin did as she was told. As soon as the leash snapped into place, Blue stood at attention.

"Good!" John seemed pleased though Erin wasn't sure why.

The time went quickly. Erin learned all about the basic gaiting patterns. She walked Blue in a circle, in a triangle, in a straight line, even in something John called an L pattern. She learned that Blue was supposed to walk slightly in front of her, at the end of the leash. She also learned that she had to be firm with Blue.

"Blue!" She reprimanded as he tried to pull away and chase after the birds. He'd been trying to run after the birds all morning. She jerked on the leash. Blue ignored her. "Woof! Woof!" The birds scattered into the sky. Blue shot after them so quickly that Erin was almost pulled off her feet. "Hey!" She laughed.

"Remember," John reminded her, "while you're holding the end of that leash, you're in charge. And keep your voice stern. Blue has to know you mean business. This isn't playtime."

She nodded. Working with Blue was a lot harder than she'd thought it would be.

"Hang in there," John encouraged. "You can't expect perfection the first time you step into the ring. It's going to take time." John motioned for the L pattern and with a sigh Erin brought Blue back into position.

The lesson was almost over when Erin noticed her grandmother returning from the kennel with Abby. Expecting Blue to chase after the small dog, she stopped what she was doing and clenched the leash tightly in her hand. The Lab stopped too and immediately gave her a puzzled look.

"Keep gaiting him. Put him through his paces," John instructed. Abby's yipping and yapping grew louder as Grandma approached. "This is all part of the process," John continued. "There will be lots of other dogs at the show and Blue has to get used to the distraction. So do you." Erin began to walk with Blue again and, aside from a long look as he passed Abby, the black Lab kept going.

Behind her, Erin could hear her grandmother trying to control the beagle. "Abby, no!" Grandma spoke sternly to the dog. "Quiet." When the beagle stopped braying, she reached into her pocket and rewarded her with a dog treat. "Good girl," Peggy praised. "Good girl!"

By the time Erin completed one last circuit with Blue, Cassie was standing with her grandmother, laughing at Abbey's antics. When the beagle wasn't twisting and jumping for attention, she was trying to get her long nose into Grandma's pocket, where the dog treats were kept. Erin smiled and was about to call a greeting, but John stopped her. "Ignore Cassie for now, Erin. Just like Blue has to ignore other dogs, you have to ignore other people," he explained mildly. "Blue takes his cues from you. If you're not paying attention, he won't, either."

Erin knew John wasn't angry — he was simply stating a fact — but she flushed with embarrassment, then forced herself to ignore Cassie and kept on going. She seemed to be making one mistake after another!

"We'll do more tomorrow," John unsnapped Blue's leash. Tail wagging, the Lab immediately ran toward Abby. "It's almost lunchtime and I know you and Cassie have plans."

They *did* have plans. Big plans. They were spending the afternoon at Stoton Falls. And that meant music and secrets and their first picnic lunch. With lots and lots of food.

"I don't know which one I like more," Cassie said when Erin joined her. "Abby or Blue. Look at them. They're both so cute!"

She watched the two dogs play a game of chase. When they came together, their mouths would open and playfully they would wrestle. "I still like Blue," Erin declared. She giggled as Abby got hold of Blue's ear and wouldn't let go.

"How did it go, darlin'?"

"Well," Erin admitted, glancing at her grandmother, "it wasn't as easy as I thought."

"Time and practice," John reassured her. "That's all you need."

Blue barked at Abby and the beagle howled in answer. Grandma checked her watch. "I should put that one back in her kennel," she said. "It's almost time for lunch."

The two girls exchanged looks. Lunch! Time to go! "I brought the radio," Cassie whispered to Erin. "And leftover pizza, pasta salad, and two kinds of crackers. Do you have some of that shortcake?"

"Yep. And cold chicken, veggies and dip, and a thermos of grape punch." Erin turned to her grandmother. "Grandma," she asked. "Do you think I could. . .?"

"If this is about bringing Abby inside the house, don't even think of it." Her grandmother gave her a mock frown. "Just look what happened when I let Blue come inside. If you had your way, the whole kennel would be in my living room." She gave Erin an exasperated sigh, but there was a twinkle in her brown eyes.

"No, Grandma, that's not it," Erin laughed. "We're off for our swim and I want to take Blue with me." The words rushed out but she couldn't stop them. "I can put him on the springer and he'll run along beside me. He'll be fine. I know he will." She didn't want to be away from Blue even for a minute.

Grandma shook her head. "Not today, Erin."

"Blue's tired," John said. "He had a good run before we started working with him. He needs time to rest."

Blue didn't look very tired to her, she thought, watching the Lab and the beagle wrestle on the grass. He had more energy than she did.

"Another day," Grandma promised.

"Besides, we have *plans* to make, remember?" Cassie hissed in her ear. "Reinvention plans."

"Oh, that." Erin reached for the knapsack she had left in the shade of the apple tree and led the way to the shed where her bike was stored. "I'm not sure about that anymore."

Cassie's face fell. She watched while Erin went inside and searched for her bike. "Why not?" she called after her.

Silently Erin wheeled the bike out from the shed. In the distance she could see Blue's tail droop as her grandmother led his playmate off to the kennel. She giggled softly before turning to Cassie. "I don't think I'm going to have time." Her old helmet was dusty and she gave it a wipe. "Training Blue is going to be way harder than I thought it would be. Plus John says I have to learn about dog anatomy and how to groom him. And Duchess is having puppies." She shook her head. "There's just a lot going on this summer. I'm not going to have time to worry about warts and hair and stuff like that."

Cassie got on her bike. "Then let me worry about it." The two girls headed down the driveway. "Me and Treena."

They cycled past the holly and turned right on Dove Creek Road. They had a long ride ahead of them before they even reached the old logging road that would take them to the falls. But there was just enough wind in the air to cool Erin off and memories of the rushing water and the slick, black rocks that would be waiting for them at the end of their ride encouraged her to pedal quickly and steadily.

She didn't need a reinvention. Not now that she was away from Deryk Latham and his calls of Beauty and the Beast. Not now that she was far away from bakeries and girls who teased her about baboon legs. She had too much work to do. Besides, her mother was right. She was perfect as she was. Warts and all.

"Come on," she yelled over her shoulder to Cassie, "race you!"

6

Stoton Falls was one of Erin's all-time favorite places. In the winter when the water level rose and the Puntledge River turned cold and deep, it swept away their picnic spots. But when the water receded in summer, it exposed more than a mile of black slate slabs scattered through the water like chocolate discs on a great big birthday cake.

Erin and Cassie carefully picked their way through the shallows of the river, pushing their bikes over and around the rocks. The mossy surfaces were slippery and the bikes were heavy. Small waterfalls trickled over their feet and licked at Erin's rolled-up jeans. Around them groups of kids laughed and splashed. The girls kept their eyes down, careful not to step into one of the tiny swimming holes that sat just below the surface. Some were shallow but many were not.

They were heading for the base of the big waterfall, just past the rock formation they called the dinosaur spine, to their special spot on the marshmallow rocks. In her haste to get around the final turn to the fossil wall and "their" spot, Erin almost slipped. Grabbing at her bike, she caught herself just in time. With a triumphant smile directed at Cassie, she pushed her bike past a mother and young child, and rounded the corner.

Treena was there, stretched out on *their* rock, her pale body slick with suntan lotion. She waved a languid hand in greeting and silently turned back to her book. Erin frowned and turned questioning eyes to Cassie, but her friend gave her a silent shrug. First-of-the-summer picnics were almost always just for the two of them. They had so much catching up to do.

They leaned their bikes against the slate wall, retrieved their packs, and slowly made their way through the water to a nearby rock. Erin laid down the familiar red plaid blanket and glanced around. Three boys chiseled for fossils nearby. A group of kids laughed as they rode over the falls in an inner tube. She'd forgotten how loud the waterfall was. Even with Treena nearby, she and Cassie should be able to talk easily without being overheard.

"I'm going swimming before I eat." She unzipped her jeans and eyed the big pool at the base of the falls. There were a few kids playing around the edge, but the middle was empty. She couldn't wait to cool off.

"What do you think?" Cassie was one step ahead of her. She flung her shorts and T-shirt into a heap and posed on the blanket with one arm on her hip and the other behind her head. "Like it?"

She was referring to her new bathing suit. It was bubble gum pink. But it wasn't the color that caught Erin's eye — it was Cassie's body inside the bikini. Cassie had developed breasts. Just like Rachel.

"Nice," Erin mumbled, suddenly self-conscious of the way she looked. She must be the only flat-chested twelve-year-old on the planet! Even the new bathing suit didn't make her feel any better. It had looked great at the store but now, beside Cassie's flashy pink one, it was pretty boring.

She turned away. She took her time folding her jeans before reluctantly pulling her shirt over her head. Carefully she folded it too and placed everything in a neat little pile. By the time she was done, Cassie was paddling in the swimming hole.

"Come on!" her friend yelled. "Don't be such a slowpoke."

The first rush of cold water took her breath away. Cassie splashed her and Erin's discomfort faded. So what if Cassie was developing? She *was* a whole year older. She splashed her friend back and dunked her head below the water. It felt good to cool off after that workout session with Blue and the long bike ride.

More than an hour passed before Treena called out. She was lonely and hungry, she said. By then, Erin was too hungry to care how she looked in her suit.

"This is some kind of spread." Treena grinned and

unwrapped wedges of cheese, grapes, and vegetable turnovers — her contribution to their lunch. "There's enough here for six."

Cassie flopped down beside her sister and flicked on the radio. "If Chad shows up, we'll need enough for six," she said, grabbing a chicken leg and biting into it. "Can you hear that?" She gestured to the radio.

"No," Erin and Treena responded in unison. Every year Cassie insisted on bringing the radio in spite of the fact that it couldn't be heard over the falls.

Erin pulled the plaid blanket close to the two girls before helping herself to a slice of ham and pineapple pizza and a carrot stick. "Who's Chad?" she asked.

"Treena's boyfriend." Cassie gave Erin a sly grin. She licked some barbecue sauce from her fingers.

"He's not my boyfriend." A lone fly buzzed close to the pasta salad and Treena shooed it away. She began putting food on a plate. Her long nails, painted fuchsia pink to match her bathing suit, gleamed in the sun.

"He's a boy and he's a friend." Cassie shrugged. "That makes him a boyfriend in my book."

Treena raised her perfectly arched eyebrows. "Then you're reading the wrong books, Cassandra," she said pointedly.

"Right," Cassie muttered sulkily. She finished her chicken and dished out some pasta salad.

Erin hid her smile behind the last of her pizza. Cassie hated being called Cassandra and Treena knew it.

"So what's new with you this year, Erin?" Treena popped a cracker into her mouth.

Erin thought right away about Beauty and the Beast

but she hesitated, not sure she was comfortable telling "Treena-the-glamor-queen" her problem.

Cassie could read her mind. "It's okay," she said. "Treena's cool."

And so Erin told her about Rachel's crush on the Oresti twins and the problem of Deryk Latham and Beauty and the Beast. She told her about winning the contest to work at the SPCA and her father losing his job and that's why she had to spend the whole summer with her grandmother.

After a few minutes, Cassie interrupted her and pointed at Treena's plate. "If you aren't going to eat that, can I have it?" She was eyeing a piece of pepperoni pizza. It was surrounded by pasta salad, two turnovers, and a huge wedge of strawberry shortcake.

"I'm just taking my time, that's all." The older girl bit into a slice of pizza. "Go on, Erin," she encouraged.

Erin continued on about acing her final exams and how her mother was teaching summer school. She talked about Duchess being pregnant and how that meant she could take Blue into the show ring. At that point, Cassie interrupted again and told her sister how she thought Erin needed a reinvention for her hair and legs and the warts on her hand.

Treena smiled and nibbled on a carrot. "Any time," she offered graciously. "Reinventions are my specialty."

"Thank you," Erin said politely. "But I —"

"I thought I smelled food." The voice was deep and full of laughter. A tall blond wearing cut-offs and a gray sweatshirt smiled at them. Actually he was smiling at Treena.

"Chad!" Treena's eyes began to shine. "Sit down and help yourself. There's lots here."

Erin glanced at the remains of their picnic. They had been so hungry they'd managed to polish off everything but a lone slice of pizza, a few crackers, traces of pasta salad, and some fruit. There wasn't much left at all.

"Here." Treena handed her overflowing plate to Chad. "I saved you some."

"Thanks." Chad sat down on the rock next to Treena. With his dark blue eyes and easy smile, he reminded Erin of her next-door neighbor, Bruce. "You sure?" He dangled his feet over the edge into a small swimming hole.

Treena nodded happily and watched him take a huge bite out of a vegetable turnover.

Erin and Cassie exchanged grins. "See?" her friend mouthed.

She nodded.

"Mark and Robert are fishing up river." Chad picked up a napkin and wiped his lips. "They'll be down after a while."

Cassie groaned. "That'll give me indigestion for sure." She grabbed the fruit and stood up. "Come on. Let's leave the lovebirds alone."

Treena's eyes flashed angrily at her sister but she said nothing. Chad was so busy eating his pizza Erin was sure he hadn't heard.

"Who are Mark and Robert?" Erin asked when they were finally settled on a nearby rock.

"Chad's brother and one of his friends," Cassie

fiddled with the radio dial. "They're real pains. Especially his brother, Mark." She was silent as she selected a station. Erin wasn't sure how Cassie could hear anything over the waterfall but eventually her friend seemed satisfied. "Even Treena agrees with me." She turned back to Erin. "The guy's got a problem."

Laughter drifted toward them and Erin glanced back at Chad and Treena. Chad had removed his shirt, and the two of them were stretched out on the blanket together sharing a drink. Erin didn't care whether Chad was Treena's boyfriend or not. She was just glad he had come because now she and Cassie could be alone, like they usually were for their first picnic of the year.

Erin and Cassie talked for the rest of the afternoon. They traded secrets and dreams. They discussed going into grade seven and what it was like getting older. They chatted about the reinvention and why Cassie liked boys. After a while Erin swallowed her shyness and told Cassie she was lucky she had breasts. Cassie told her not to worry and predicted that she would have breasts bigger than hers by next summer. They even whispered and giggled about Chad and Treena — especially when Treena put sunscreen on Chad's shoulders. They timed her. It took her four minutes and thirty-seven seconds. Probably some kind of record, Cassie suggested. And Erin had laughed so hard she'd gotten the hiccups.

They were just starting to pack up when Erin heard the voices. Cassie heard them too. "Oh no," Cassie said. "It's Mark and Robert. Hurry up. Let's go."

Cassie wrapped up the last of the fruit while Erin

grabbed the plastic containers and stuffed them into her knapsack.

"Leave some for us," yelled a miniature version of Chad. That must be Mark, Erin decided as the boy came closer. He carried a fishing rod over one shoulder and a tackle box in his free hand.

"Ya," agreed the second, who was also weighed down with fishing gear. He was shorter, with dark hair and a friendly face.

"Too late," said Treena cheerfully. "Your brother ate it all up."

"Hey!" Chad protested.

Treena giggled and gave him a friendly push. They wandered away to explore the big swimming hole at the base of the falls.

Cassie smirked. Erin picked up the blanket and gave it a shake.

"At least we're not too late for the fashion show." Mark leaped from rock to rock until he was just behind Cassie. "Whatda' ya think, Rob?" He eyed Cassie up and down. Cassie couldn't see his eyes but Erin could. He had mean eyes. Deryk Latham eyes. "In the bathing suit competition, I'd give this one an eight. How about you?"

Robert smirked and moved through the water to join Mark. "Kind of skinny," he said, hoisting his rod higher on his shoulder. "I'd say a seven."

Cassie spun around and glared at them. "Get lost," she hissed. "Nobody invited you."

"Okay, okay." Mark held up his hands and grinned. "An eight point five. The bathing suit's nice. Real nice." His eyes skimmed Cassie. "Another year or two and you'll look as good as her." He jerked his head toward the falls where Treena and Chad were splashing each other.

"Come on, Cass," Erin threw a corner of the blanket at her friend. "Help me so we can get out of here."

"Don't be in such a hurry." Mark's eyes turned to Erin. "The competition's not over yet."

The girls began to fold the blanket. Mark jumped over two rocks to get behind Erin. She could feel his eyes on her neck, her suit, the back of her legs. Why hadn't they gotten dressed before they started cleaning up?

"This one's not going to make it," Mark said to Robert. "Not in that old lady bathing suit. Nice hair though. Especially on her legs." He hooted. There was a burst of nervous laughter from Robert.

Erin clenched her teeth and stared at Cassie. She would not blush. She would not. Her friend shot a murderous look in the direction of Erin's shoulder. "Shut up, Mark," Cassie warned.

Mark ignored her. "I'd say a three, Robert. Whatda'ya think? Hmm?" He didn't wait for Robert's answer. "She might do better in the talent competition, though. Especially if she could do an ape call or two. How 'bout it, Ape Woman? What do you think?"

The two boys broke into hysterical laughter.

Erin's face flamed. Her mouth filled with a sharp, bitter taste. The taste of humiliation. She pulled the blanket from Cassie and jammed it into her pack. Grabbing her jeans and shirt from the rock, she shoved them on top. Forget about getting dressed. She was going home right now! In her bathing suit.

Quickly she marched the few feet to her bike. She didn't bother looking down or even worrying about her footing. She didn't care if she fell into a swimming hole. Maybe if she was lucky, it would be big enough to swallow her right up.

Cassie came to Erin's rescue just like Rachel did when Deryk Latham got nasty. "At least apes have brains," she yelled over her shoulder as she joined Erin by the bikes. "Unlike the two of you."

Mark hooted again but Robert was silent.

"Ignore him," Cassie said with a frown. "Like I said before, he has a problem." She pulled her shirt over her head and picked up her shorts.

A problem. Right. Just like Deryk Latham and those girls at the bakery. Just like half the kids at school. "I'm going!" Erin turned her bike to the river and pushed it through the shallows.

But Cassie was already zipping up her shorts. "I'm ready." She slung her knapsack over her shoulder and grabbed her bike. "Wait for me."

"Hey, you guys!" Treena yelled from the river.

But Erin and Cassie didn't answer. They didn't even glance back. Instead they slipped and slithered as fast as they dared over the mossy rocks that would take them away from Stoton Falls and back to the safety and silence of Dove Creek Kennels.

7

Erin waved to Cassie and slowly wheeled her bike toward the shed. There was a car in her grandmother's driveway — a navy blue sedan parked beyond the holly in the shade of the evergreen tree. Her grandmother had company. Good! She'd be too busy to talk. Erin just wanted to hide.

Quietly she let herself into the kitchen. She could hear her grandmother talking in the living room. If she was lucky, she could tiptoe down the hall to her bedroom where she could pull the blankets over her head and forget all about apes and beauty contests and horrible boys named Mark.

But Erin hadn't counted on Blue.

He heard the door creak. With a welcoming woof, he

bounded out from the living room and threw himself at her, his tongue playing over her cheek and down her chin.

"Okay, okay!" Erin dropped to her knees, wrapped her arms around his neck, and buried her face in his black fur. Blue didn't care what she looked like. He loved her no matter what.

"Is that you, m'darlin'?" her grandmother called.

So much for hiding! "It's me." She gave Blue's haunches one last rub before going into the living room. "I'm still in my bathing suit," she apologized, self-conscious all over again of the hair on her legs, her height, the plain blue suit.

"Doesn't matter." Grandma smiled. "Come and meet Sheila Jones." She gestured to the plump woman sitting on the chair opposite. Cups and a plate of cookies were scattered on the coffee table between them. "She's an old friend and interested in buying one of Duchess's puppies."

"Hello." Erin stood awkwardly in the doorway and nodded at the woman. She was almost formal, in a blue dress, high heels, and a small hat. Quite out of character for most of her grandmother's friends, who favored jeans and sweats.

"How delightful to meet you." Sheila Jones beamed. "I knew your father when he was your age. You look just like him."

Great. Now she looked like a fifty-one-year-old man. She tried to smile. "I really should get dressed." She glanced longingly down the hall as she tried to excuse herself.

"Nonsense," Sheila Jones responded heartily. "You look lovely. I must say it's terribly refreshing to see a young person wearing an appropriate swimming costume. So many of them these days appear almost naked. It's quite frightful, really. But you look very respectable." She nodded approvingly. "I could almost see myself wearing something like that."

Suddenly Erin hated her navy blue bathing suit. Her old lady suit. That's what Mark had called it. And Mark had been right.

Her grandmother caught Erin's eye and gave her a wink. Don't mind her, Grandma seemed to be saying.

She took a step backward, ready to bolt down the hall to the safety of her bedroom.

But Sheila Jones wasn't finished yet. "Yes, you do look like your father when he was a child. Only much prettier, of course." She turned to Erin's grandmother. "I must say, old girl, you do know how to turn them out. Beautiful children and beautiful dogs." She chuckled at her own joke. "You've got that standard of perfection down to a T."

I'm perfect, all right, Erin thought. Perfectly awful.

Sheila Jones turned back to Erin. "I understand you're taking Blue into the ring this summer." She clasped her hands together. "When I judged dog shows, the look of the handler was just as important as the look of the dog. You have such a pretty smile and . . . well, your posture needs work . . . but if you improve that, I'm sure you'll score highly. Very highly indeed." She repeated herself.

Mrs. Jones needed to work on keeping her mouth

shut, Erin thought crossly.

"Of course, keeping control of the dog is important, too, but you look like a big, strong girl," Mrs. Jones gushed. "I'm sure you'll do fine."

Now she was a big, strong girl who looked like a fifty-one-year-old man or maybe an ape woman, depending on your point of view. This was not her day.

"Go ahead and dress, darlin'." Grandma must have sensed that Erin yearned to escape. "We won't be long here."

"Not at all," Sheila added. "I was just telling your grandmother that I want another yellow Labrador just like my Radcliffe. The best of the litter, he was. A show dog if there ever was one. And that's what I'm looking for again. Another one that meets the standard of perfection for the breed."

"Of course." Grandma straightened in her chair. "You know I pride myself on the lines I breed. The aim, of course, is the best possible puppies. As close to perfection as possible."

"Wonderful." Sheila nodded vigorously.

"Duchess was paired with a sire from Milwaukee," Grandma continued. "An outstanding dog really. They make a fabulous match. I'm expecting the entire litter to be show material. I'm sure you'll be completely satisfied."

Erin fled. Down the hall she raced, grabbing the portable phone as she went. She was used to her grandmother's practicality when it came to her breeding program, but all of a sudden it hit her. Standard of perfection. That was her problem. She didn't have one.

And if they were going to be judging the way she looked in the ring, she was in big trouble.

Her grandmother didn't tolerate imperfections in her pups. Oh sure, she loved them all and she made sure they all had very good homes, but Erin knew her heart was with those puppies that had the standard of perfection down to a T.

Blue was one of them. He would be perfect at the dog show. Just perfect. But she wouldn't be! And she would be right beside him. Ruining his chances to come in first.

Quickly Erin dialed the familiar number. Her dad had said she was perfect the way she was. Well, he was wrong. She wasn't perfect . . . but she could be better. A lot better. She had to be for the sake of the dog show. For Blue. And to stop people like Deryk and Mark and girls with Vuarnet sunglasses from talking about her. Stop them once and for all.

She listened to the phone on the other end ringing. Impatiently Erin tapped her fingers on the bedspread. "Hurry up and answer Cassie," she spoke out loud. "The on-again, off-again reinvention is definitely on!"

* * * *

Erin stared at the list in front of her.

"Well?" Cassie leaned across her kitchen table and tapped the paper with a slim blue pen. "What do you think?"

"It looks pretty good." She sipped her root beer and read the list again. *Pluck eyebrows. Fix hair. Shave legs.*

Get rid of warts on knuckle. Buy new clothes. And a new bathing suit. Learn to walk without tripping. It was a lot to do, but they had almost a month until the dog show. "I'm still not sure about shaving," she admitted finally. "My mom did say no."

Cassie's eyes flashed with annoyance. "That was before Mark said all those awful things to you," she pointed out. "I'm sure she'd change her mind now."

Their picnic was four days ago but Erin could hear Mark's words like he was yelling them from Cassie's living room. Ape Woman. An old lady bathing suit. A *three*.

"I guess."

"How about we leave the legs for now and start with your hair? Or your warts?"

She brightened. "My warts," she said firmly. "Let's do those first."

Cassie grabbed Erin's hand and studied her knuckles. "Maybe we could just cut them off?" she suggested.

Erin pulled her hand back. "No way." She gave Cassie a sheepish grin. "Besides, I tried it a few months ago. It didn't work."

"I read a book about spells once and it said you could rub all sorts of things on warts to make them go away," Cassie said.

"Like what?"

"Toenails. Garlic. Even Pepsi."

Erin wrinkled her nose. "Gross. I thought you said your mom has some wart stuff?" Cassie's mom wasn't the natural medicine nut Erin's mother was.

"Right!" Cassie stood up and pushed her chair back. "Come on."

Cassie's bathroom was cheerful and cluttered. It had blue and white towels, a shower curtain covered with brightly colored fish, and a vanity that held bottles of hand cream and perfume. It wasn't particularly large, but it gave Cassie and Erin just enough room to move.

"Here it is." Cassie pulled a tiny bottle filled with clear liquid from the cupboard. "Wart Away." She began to read the fine print on the back. "It says to use it every day for a week and then stop." She looked at Erin. "You'll have to take it home," she said. "Or else come over every day."

Erin grinned and nodded. Finally her warts would be gone!

"Are you ready?" Cassie asked as she unscrewed the cap.

She nodded a second time. No more crater claw for her. She held out her hand and watched as Cassie filled the dropper full of the clear liquid and positioned it over the bigger wart.

Drip. Drip.

"Oww!" She flinched.

"Sit still!" Cassie ordered. "I haven't gotten the second one yet."

"But it stings!" Erin jerked her hand away and eyed the tiny bottle of Wart Away on Cassie's bathroom counter. "I think it's going to eat through my entire hand." She stared nervously at the warts on her knuckle.

"It's perfectly safe," Cassie reassured her. "Come on, let me get them."

"OWWWWW!" Erin waved her hand madly in the air. "It stings, Cass. Real bad." She clenched her teeth.

Cassie stared at her. "Your face is turning red. I've never seen you—"

"It HURTS!" Erin screamed. "Turn on the water."

Cassie did.

Erin stuck her hand under the tap. Immediate relief. "I'm not using that again," she said when the stinging finally subsided. "No wonder my mom hates chemicals. We'll have to find something else."

Cassie replaced the lid on the bottle of Wart Away and tucked it back into the cupboard. "How about the garlic?" she suggested.

Erin slid off the bathroom counter and stood on the floor. "The garlic sounds pretty stupid," she said. "I can't believe it'll work."

"It's worth a try," Cassie said. "Come on."

Into the kitchen they went. The early afternoon sun streamed through the windows and turned the pine cabinets a pretty golden yellow. Copper pots hung on the wall beside the fridge. A small clay crock to the left of the stove held one fat shallot and several heads of garlic. Cassie began rolling one of the heads on the counter.

"What are you doing?" Erin glanced nervously toward the living room where she could hear Cassie's mother talking to Treena. Thank goodness they hadn't heard her screaming in the bathroom.

"I'm loosening them." Cassie peeled away the silvery paper and pulled two cloves from the bulb. She grabbed a knife from the drawer and began to cut. "Now the book says to rub the warts with the cloves and then plant the cloves somewhere in the garden. When the clove dies, the wart will shrivel up, too."

It was silly but Erin was willing to try anything. Anything that didn't hurt, that is. "What if the clove grows?" she wondered out loud. "Does that mean my wart grows bigger?"

"Cloves don't grow," Cassie said matter-of-factly. "Would anything that smells this bad want to grow bigger?" She held the cut clove under Erin's nose.

Erin sniffed. "I guess not," she said. "What kind of book was this in again?"

"A book on magic spells." Cassie reached for Erin's hand. "I got it out of the library when I was trying to get Jonathan to like me." She held out the cut clove. "Stand still while I rub." She hesitated. "I think I'm supposed to say a spell or something. I can't remember."

There was movement in the living room. It sounded like Treena and Cassie's mother were coming into the kitchen. "Hurry up!" Erin whispered. "Just make something up."

"Okay!" Cassie squeezed her eyes shut. "Wart no, wart flow. With this clove I make you go." Quickly she rubbed the garlic back and forth over Erin's warts. "Go, wart, go."

"What are you girls doing in here?" Cassie's mother smiled at them from the doorway.

"Nothing," Erin and Cassie said in unison. Cassie folded her fist around the clove of garlic and tucked it behind her back.

"Smells like Caesar salad in here," Treena opened the fridge and peered inside. "But it's too early for salad, I'm still looking for breakfast."

Erin giggled nervously but Cassie frowned. "We're going outside now." She pulled Erin toward the back door. "Bye."

"You've got a mess to clean up," her mother called after her.

"Later," Cassie yelled back.

They wandered away from the house, beyond the flower fields, to a shady corner near some dark red poppies. "We'll plant the clove here," Cassie told Erin, "and when it turns to mush, your wart will, too!"

Erin crouched and started to dig a little hole. "I wonder how long it'll take?"

"Longer than a week," Cassie predicted as she helped dig. "I think that's big enough." She tossed in the clove of garlic and began to cover it with soil. "I have to say another spell," she told Erin.

A seagull screeched overhead. Erin jumped. In spite of the warm afternoon sun, she felt cold. The garlic idea had seemed goofy at first, but now it seemed almost spooky. She rubbed nervously at the warts on her knuckle. "Okay," she agreed.

Cassie stared silently at the ground. Finally she looked up. "Got it," she said confidently. Ceremoniously she held a handful of soil above the small hole.

"Rot, clove, rot. Go, wart, go. And as you rot, the wart will go." Slowly she let the stream of soil fall. "There!" Cassie patted the ground triumphantly. "You just wait, Erin. Those warts will disappear and you'll never know you had them!"

"I hope so!" Erin watched the seagull glide on the wind before it turned in a slow arc and headed south. She and Cassie followed it.

Cassie gave her a sly grin. "And you wait," she said. "The perfect reinvention is just beginning."

Erin grinned back. Her uneasy feeling was gone. Cassie was right! By the time the dog show rolled around, she'd be the perfect Erin Morris. To go with the perfect Mr. Lavender Blue.

"Today your warts, tomorrow the rest of you."

Erin held out her left hand and stared at her knuckles. Was it her imagination or were the warts already looking smaller? "The rest of me is going to have to wait awhile," she told Cassie. "I've got to train some more with Blue. And then there's clothes shopping to do. For the show." She stopped by her bike. "Maybe you could come," she said, "and help me pick some stuff out."

"Great!" Cassie loved shopping. "When?"

"I'm going to be busy training this weekend," Erin said, "so sometime next week. Maybe Tuesday or Wednesday. I'll call you."

"We'll get you a new bathing suit," Cassie said excitedly. "And some cute little tops and —"

"I'm not putting on another bathing suit this summer!" She reached for her helmet and pulled it on.

"Once you shave your legs, you'll feel different," Cassie predicted.

She snapped the helmet strap in place. "I told you when we made the list, I'm still not sure about shaving my legs." She remembered Mark's taunts at the river a few days ago. Maybe she should defy her mother's wishes and shave them anyway. Like Cassie said, the hair was bound to grow back by the time she went home at the end of summer. Still, the idea of sneaking around behind her mother's back made her feel kind of creepy inside.

Cassie grinned and that mischievous look sparkled in her eyes. "We'll figure something out," she yelled as Erin swung her leg over her bike and pushed off toward her grandmother's house. "See you soon."

8

"Look what came in the mail." John waved an envelope at Erin when she walked through the door of the kennel the following Wednesday. "A registration form for the Campbell River dog show. It's running a week after the one in Comox. Interested?"

Erin handed John the warm muffins her grandmother had sent out from the kitchen. "Don't think so." She took a blueberry muffin and perched on a stool to eat it. That daydream about getting her name in the paper and having people calling to walk their dogs was just a daydream. A daydream that didn't matter. All that mattered was getting her own dog.

John put the envelope down. He turned back to the stainless steel bowl where he was mixing up breakfast meal. The dogs were hungry. Abby was howling. Butch was pacing. Pharaoh and Star were throwing themselves against the cage with solid thuds.

Erin was still trying to wake up. Her grandmother had gotten her up early and said she had a lot to learn today.

"Why not?" John asked.

Erin shrugged. She wasn't sure the perfect reinvention would be perfect enough but she couldn't tell John that. "One show's probably enough for me." She bit into a blueberry and the warm juice filled her mouth.

"The more shows you do, the more points you accumulate. And the more exposure Blue gets, the better it is for your grandmother."

She reached out and scratched Blue behind his ear. The dog ignored her. His brown eyes were fixed firmly on the muffin in her other hand. "I know," she said. But it would only take one show to prove to her parents that she was responsible enough for a dog. Especially if Blue won. Correction, *when* he won.

"If you get enough points, you could find yourself at the nationals in Ottawa later this year."

"I'd have to get to the provincials first. And do a lot of dog shows." Do them well, too, Erin added silently.

John nodded and began filling individual bowls. "True enough. But I have a friend in West Vancouver who can't show his dog on his own anymore. Has a bad hip. He's looking for someone to take his shepherd on the circuit." He took Abby her food first. When he returned, he said, "Why don't you enter Blue in the

Campbell River show? You can always decide later if you want to go in."

Erin handed Blue the last piece of her muffin. The dog practically inhaled it before licking her fingers in search of more crumbs. She giggled as his tongue methodically traveled between her fingers and across her palm. Blue was the best. He deserved to be a champion. A champion twice. And maybe that daydream about getting her name in the paper wasn't a bad one, after all. "Okay," Erin said. "I'll do it."

"Good!" John gave her a pleased grin. He handed her a few sheets of paper. "Read these over while I hand out breakfast. Then we'll get to work."

"You mean I have to know all of this?" she asked John when he finished the feedings. There was so much material; Erin was worried she wouldn't remember it all. There were sheets on the history of her breed, the rules of the show ring, and photographs of proper form.

"The judges are going to question you about your breed. You never know what they're going to ask, so all you can do is be prepared. Don't worry," John reassured her, "lots of this stuff you already know."

"Lots of it I don't." She re-read the section on characteristics. "I didn't know Labs have a double coat." She flipped to health. "And I've heard Grandma talk about hip dysplasia, but I didn't know about ear infections. Or skin allergies."

John grabbed a stool of his own and sat beside Erin. "By the time I'm finished with you, you'll know it all."

She looked glum.

"It's all part of the show prep." John's voice was soft but firm. "You're Blue's handler. You're being judged even more than the dog. It's a feather in your grand-mother's cap if Blue does well, but he doesn't have to be a top dog. You, on the other hand, need to understand your breed and learn to handle your dog perfectly."

And look good, Erin added silently.

John reached for the papers in her hand. "We'll start with Labrador history," he said.

* * * *

Erin was surprised to learn that she *did* know a lot about Labrador retrievers. What she didn't know, John explained. He was a good teacher and he made learning fun. It helped that Blue was with them. When some-thing needed explaining, they had the perfect model right at hand. Time went very fast. Erin was shocked when John glanced at his watch and told her more than an hour had gone by. After a long stretch and another muffin, they started in on grooming techniques.

"Show Blue the brush," John instructed. She held the black-handled brush below Blue's nose. He sniffed curiously at the yellow bristles. "That way he knows it's time to be groomed," John explained. He gave Blue a scratch behind his ears before he turned to leave. "Just remember what I said. Start at the top of the head and work back. Pay attention to the undercoat, espe-cially around his neck. Call me when you're done."

Blue's eyes followed John as he walked to Abby's cage and let the small dog out.

"Okay, Blue." Gently Erin began to brush the top of Blue's head. The dog tossed her hand off with the flick of his long, black nose. His tongue came out and licked her knuckles. Her warty, crater claw knuckles. "Stop it!" She tried to frown but she giggled instead. Again his tongue licked her warts. "Blue!" It had been five days since she and Cassie had buried the clove of garlic. The warts looked just the same to her but no matter how many times she washed her left hand, Blue had developed a real taste for it.

"Be firm," John yelled out. "You're in charge, remember." He was brushing Abby.

"That's it, Blue." She gave the dog a pretend fierce frown. "Sit still and let me groom you." With firm strokes she began to brush. Blue sensed that she meant business. Finally he was still. The only movement was the blinking of his dark eyes as he watched her.

He was so gorgeous, with his large, square head and his jet black fur. It was impossible to stay mad at him. Even pretend mad. She lifted his head and began on his neck. Blue closed his eyes in pleasure.

Erin tasted caramel apple happiness. For a minute she pretended Blue was her dog; that he would be going home with her after her time in Courtenay. She could see exactly how it would be.

Her father would pull the car onto the deck of the ferry. Her parents would gather their magazines as they prepared to get out. I'm going to stay below deck, Erin would say. With Blue. Her parents would give her an approving nod and Erin would settle down with a book. But she would have no time to read, because the men who worked the ferry would stop by the car every few minutes to comment on the ribbons her dog wore around his neck. She would introduce him. Mr. Lavender Blue, she would say. A champion. First prize in two dog shows. And when she was home and Rachel and the Oresti twins came over and saw Blue lying on the rug in her living room, she would —

Something cold touched Erin's wrist. She jumped; the brush almost flew from her hand. It was Abby, wagging her tail and checking things out.

"How are you doing?" John asked a minute later. He crouched down and watched her move from Blue's stomach to his haunches. "Looking good," he said approvingly. "When you finish up, I'll show you how to clean his teeth."

"I don't have to do *that* at the show, do I?"

John laughed. "No," he reassured her. "But the judge sometimes wants to look in the dog's mouth. Blue hates having anyone messing around in there. He needs to get used to it."

Erin nodded and began working on Blue's tail.

Abby put her head between her paws and stuck her bum in the air. "Woof!" The beagle thought it was playtime. She was trying to get Blue's attention. "You sit," John ordered. Surprisingly, the beagle did exactly as she was told. "I hear your grandmother has a shopping trip planned for this afternoon." John's eyes twinkled.

She wrinkled her nose. "At least Cassie's coming." On the phone last night Cassie had made the shopping trip sound almost fun.

"Looks like they're pretty anxious to get going." John pointed. Cassie and Grandma were coming through the door. "We'll have to leave the teeth for another day," he said.

"Hi!" Erin grinned and put down the brush. Blue gave a shake of pleasure at being free. Abby began running circles around the two women.

"Hello, darlin'." Grandma moved swiftly through the kennel, reaching out to give the beagle an absent-minded pat. "How's Duchess?"

"She's been really quiet this morning," John responded. "Wouldn't even eat her breakfast."

"Did you bring your money?" Erin whispered as Cassie joined her.

Cassie nodded and the two girls walked toward Duchess's cage. "Mom gave me my allowance early," she whispered back. "You should see my list. It's huge."

"Her time might be coming close," John was saying to Grandma when the two girls caught up. Blue was ahead of them, sticking his nose into the cage and whining softly at Duchess.

"When is she due?" Cassie asked.

"Not for another nine days," Grandma said, unlocking the door. Blue rushed in ahead of her, nudged Duchess with the tip of his nose before lying down close beside her. "Look out, Blue." Grandma gave him a gentle push. "Give me some room." Blue stood up, turned in a half circle, and settled down with a "thrump" only a few inches away from Duchess.

Grandma sighed in exasperation but her lips

twitched. Stretching past Blue, she began palpating Duchess's stomach. The yellow Lab raised her head and then, as if the effort to keep it in the air was simply too much, she put it back down again. "I can feel five," Grandma said after a minute. "Maybe even six." She rocked back on her heels and glanced at the food and water dishes before turning her eyes back to Duchess. "Everything seems fine but I'd feel better if you'd eat something, Duchess, old girl." She gave Duchess one last rub on her belly before standing up. "Keep an eye on her, John. And keep her water dish full, would you?"

He nodded and hustled Abby back to her pen.

Grandma checked her watch. "We shouldn't be more than a few hours."

* * * *

"I'm sure we'll find something in this store," Grandma assured the girls as she pushed open the door to Alesa's Closet and strode inside.

Erin and Cassie followed. Within seconds Cassie was shifting her parcels from one hip to the other as she inspected a rack of skirts. Her grandmother was talking to a tall woman who had towering black hair and matching black eyebrows that sat in perfect half moons over her eyes. Erin spotted a chair near the back of the store. Finally a chance to sit down!

The chair was small and hard but it felt wonderful to her. She was tired. She was thirsty. And her feet hurt. She loosened the lace on her running shoe and rubbed her heel. She should have worn socks. She was starting a blister.

"I knew we'd find something here." Her grandmother's face was flushed with success as she joined Erin. "Alesandra has a number of outfits she thinks would work in the ring. She's going to bring them out."

"Would you mind standing, darling? I must get your size." Alesandra had an accent that reminded Erin of her Hungarian neighbor, Mrs. Czas. Reluctantly she stood. She pretended to feel patient while the woman took her measurements. Her huge black hair bobbed and dipped with each movement. Finally she was through. "I will only be a moment." She disappeared through a beaded curtain.

"Will you look at this!" Cassie shoved a bright red shirt under Erin's nose. "It's on sale for $15 and it's my size." She fumbled in one of her bags before pulling out the shorts she'd bought three stores ago. "Don't you think it would go great with these?"

Erin nodded and feigned enthusiasm. She began rubbing the heel on her other foot.

Grandma reached for Cassie's find and rubbed it between her fingers. "That's a good-quality cotton." She held it against the new shorts and eyed it critically. "It's not my taste, of course, putting red and yellow together, but I must admit it does pack a punch. At that price you can hardly lose. Why don't you try it on?" she encouraged Cassie with a smile.

"I will!"

I must be the only girl on all of Vancouver Island

who hates shopping, Erin thought glumly as she watched her grandmother take Cassie's parcels and shoo her into the dressing room.

"Now then." Alesandra was back. She hung half a dozen items on a rack and began arranging them according to color. Erin studied the woman's hair and tried to decide if it was a wig or if it was real.

"That navy blue set looks lovely, doesn't it, Erin?" Her grandmother didn't wait for an answer. Instead she played with the fabric and asked Alesandra about cleaning instructions.

Navy blue. Erin had decided she would die before she'd ever wear anything else that was navy blue. She shoved her foot back into her runner and winced as the blistered skin rubbed against the canvas.

"What do you think?" Cassie twirled in front of her. She'd put on her new yellow shorts as well. Erin had to agree with her grandmother. Together the red and yellow were Day-Glo bright. But on Cassie it looked just right.

"It looks great," she said sulkily. "It really does." Maybe she was just a boring navy blue kind of person.

Cassie studied Erin for a minute and then she knelt down beside her. "What's wrong? You're so quiet all of a sudden."

Erin shrugged. "Tired, I guess."

"You need to buy something. That'll make you feel better. Trust me." Cassie turned and eyed the rack of clothes. "Your grandma's right. They have great stuff here. I'm sure you'll find something."

Erin did. But it wasn't the same thing her grandmother liked. "Please, Grandma. Can't we get this?" Erin turned to the right and watched in the mirror as the soft flare of the white hipster pants moved with her. She smoothed the vest top and pulled her shoulders back. "I think it would look great in the ring."

Cassie gave her the thumbs-up sign but her grandmother sighed and turned troubled eyes to Alesandra. "I really wanted something more feminine." She pointed to the navy skirt set. "Something like that."

"I won't wear navy," Erin said flatly.

Cassie was waving her arms madly in the air. Don't be so disagreeable, she seemed to be saying.

But Erin was tired of being agreeable. Tired of being dragged from one store to another. Tired of trying to find just the perfect outfit to wear in the ring. It was enough that she was going to be perfect herself with the perfect reinvention. But she couldn't very well tell her grandmother that. Not yet. And not now. Not with Alesandra of the big hair watching her.

"I don't understand what it is with you and navy," her grandmother said mildly.

Erin had a brainstorm. "It's Blue," she said quickly. "He's so dark, he'd look terrible walking beside me if I was wearing navy. He'd look better if I was wearing white." She turned to the left this time and watched the bell bottoms flare out from her legs. No one would call her an old lady wearing this.

"She has a point," Alesandra said softly.

Grandma nodded. "Okay," she said slowly. "Pull out everything else in white that will fit."

"I like this, Grandma, I really do."

But her grandmother wasn't listening. She was on the phone to John, asking about Duchess and telling him they were going to be later than she'd originally thought.

Finally, after going through Alesandra's entire stock of just about everything that would fit Erin, they narrowed the choice down to three outfits: a white skirt with a multicolored top, a pale blue dress, and the white vest and pant suit Erin loved so much.

Erin eyed the white skirt nervously. It was so short. Way above her knees. "Don't you have any long white skirts?"

Alesandra shook her head. "Long skirts don't come in until fall. And then they are usually black or navy. Not white."

She couldn't wear a skirt in the ring with Blue. Erin just couldn't. Unless it was long. Or unless she defied her mother and shaved her legs like Cassie wanted her to.

"We'll be fine with one of these," Grandma said firmly. She held the blue dress against Erin and narrowed her eyes. "A little too formal, I think."

Cassie tilted her head to the side and studied Erin. "Too Alice-in-Wonderlandish."

"Oh, *heavens*, we can't have that." Grandma was clearly horrified.

Erin hid her smirk. When her grandmother turned to put the outfit back, it was her turn to give Cassie the thumbs-up sign.

"I do like this, though." Grandma held out the white skirt and bright top. "What about you, darlin'?"

In spite of the fact that the skirt was short, Erin liked the outfit, too. The skirt was a soft denim — the same fabric as the vest and pants she loved so much. The top was cut like a jacket. It was trimmed in the same white fabric but had inserts in rainbow colors. "It's nice, I guess," Erin said cautiously. "The skirt's kind of short, though."

"For heaven's sake, it's almost to your knees." Her grandmother gave Erin an exasperated look.

"What if I have to bend over in the ring or some-thing . . . ?" Erin's voice trailed away. She could tell by the look in her grandmother's eyes she had lost.

"We'll take this." Grandma handed the outfit to Alesandra. She hesitated and then reached for the white pants and vest. "You may as well wrap this up, too." She gave Erin an indulgent smile. "I'm sure you'll find a use for it sooner or later, even if you don't wear it in the ring."

Erin grinned. Her grandma was such a softie. "Thanks, Grandma." She gave her a hug.

"You're welcome, darlin'."

"Way to go," Cassie whispered to Erin as Grandma paid for the purchases. "Maybe if you work on her some more, she'll change her mind and let you wear the pants in the ring after all."

"Cassie Walker, don't you go puttin' ideas in my granddaughter's head." Grandma's voice rang out loud and clear in the small shop. "I've made my deci-sion and I'm standing by it."

"Whoops!"

Erin grinned and pulled Cassie to the front of the

store. She glanced back to her grandmother. She was intent on her conversation with Alesandra. "I'll get John to talk to her." Erin kept her voice low. "My dad says John can get her to do anything."

"What are you two giggling about?" Grandma handed Erin a large bag before opening the door and motioning them out to the sidewalk.

"Oh, nothing," Erin said with as much innocence as she could muster. Cassie's giggles grew more intense. The two girls were still laughing when they reached the car.

9

"John thinks I should wear the skirt, too." Erin shoved the last of her pepperoni pizza into her mouth and licked her fingers. Cassie's mom finished wiping the counter, reminded the girls to load their plates into the dishwasher when they were done, and wandered away. Erin picked up her mug of root beer. "I heard him tell my grandmother that proper clothing was as important as proper form." She gulped at her drink.

Cassie rolled her eyes. "It's a dog show, for heaven's sake. It's not an audience with the Queen."

Erin snorted. Some of the root beer dribbled down her chin; the rest detoured into her nose. She gasped and laughed and swallowed, all at the same time.

"That was a nose full." Cassie giggled and handed

her a tissue for her chin. But then her smile disappeared and her voice dropped. "Adults can be so weird." She jerked her head in the direction of the living room. "Like my mom and this whole makeup thing." Cassie wanted to wear lipstick and eyeshadow, but her mother wouldn't let her, even though it was summer holidays.

"What are you going to do?" Cassie asked as the two girls began to rinse their plates.

"I don't know." Erin shrugged. She stared out the kitchen window, secretly relieved to see the drizzle falling. Cassie had planned to spend this Sunday swimming at the falls. "Buy some white leotards or something." She gestured to the rain. "Looks like we'll have to stay home." Which meant she didn't have to roast at the falls in blue jeans. Because she was never putting on a bathing suit in public again.

Her friend's eyes gleamed. "Perfect! Then we have time to shave your legs." She opened the dishwasher and stacked their plates on the lower rack. "Mom bought new razors. I saw them when she unpacked the groceries last night."

Erin shook her head. "I'm not sure," she said.

"Don't be such a wimp!"

"I'm not a wimp," she said indignantly. "It's just . . . I don't know. I still have almost three weeks until the dog show. Maybe my mom will change her mind by then."

"Dream on." Cassie slammed the dishwasher. "Besides, I'm leaving in a few days to go camping for a week. That doesn't give us much time for the perfect reinvention."

"Well. . . maybe I should ask my mom again."

"And give her a chance to say no?" Cassie shook her head. "Not smart."

Erin finished her root beer and rinsed the glass. She should just do it. Pretend that she hadn't understood what her mother had said. But she had understood all too well. "Maybe I'll talk to Grandma. She'd probably understand."

"But maybe she won't," Cassie pointed out. "It's your body. You're the one who's getting teased all the time. Take some control."

"Like you're going to take control and wear lipstick and eyeshadow when your mom says no?" Erin responded hotly.

Cassie looked embarrassed. "Okay," she said reluctantly. "I see your point. Besides, if you shave now, the hair will probably grow back by show time anyway. We'll do it in August. After I get back from Long Beach."

Anything could happen by then! "Sure," Erin said.

Treena wandered into the kitchen. Rubbing sleep from her eyes, she peered blearily at Erin and Cassie. "What are you two plotting now?" she asked. Her hair was tousled, her shorts and T-shirt rumpled.

"How was your date last night with your *unboyfriend* Chad?" Cassie asked, poking Erin with her elbow. Erin swallowed her giggle.

"It wasn't a date," Treena informed her loftily. She

smoothed her blonde hair. "And there's no such word as 'unboyfriend.'" She directed a grumpy frown in the direction of the coffee pot. "What do you have to do to get a morning cup of coffee around here?"

Cassie looked at her watch and then at Erin. This time Erin couldn't help it. Her giggle slipped out. It wasn't morning anymore. She waited for Cassie to make some sarcastic remark. But Cassie surprised her.

"Sit down, Treena," Cassie said helpfully. "I'll make your coffee."

Treena slid into a chair in the nook and yawned. "Okay."

"Is it two scoops or four?" Cassie asked as she filled the kettle with hot water and put it on the stove.

"Four." Treena glanced casually at the newspaper in front of her.

Erin stared at Cassie. Cassie's eyebrows were dancing up and down, and her mouth was moving in some sort of silent message. Erin didn't get it.

"Want something to eat, Treen?" Cassie finished scooping the coffee into the cone and slid into the chair beside her sister. Erin took the chair closest to the window.

"Sure, I'll have a muffin if there's one around," Treena said casually. Slowly, her head rose from the newspaper. "What do you want, Cass?" Her blue eyes narrowed suspiciously as she studied her sister.

Cassie had the "who me?" look on her face. She made a fuss unwrapping a carrot muffin and sliding it in front of her sister. "Okay," she admitted, "I want you to cut Erin's hair."

"What?" Erin yelped.

"Erin needs her hair cut," Cassie continued.

"No, I don't!"

Cassie ignored her. "Just an inch off the bottom. You used to do mine all the time. Please, Treena?"

Treena glanced over to Erin. "Do you want your hair cut?"

Erin glared at Cassie. It was just like her friend to spring this on her with no warning at all. "No," she said defiantly. "We were going to *fix* my hair. Not cut it!"

Cassie was undeterred. "Cutting is fixing." Her face had that "I've made up my mind" look. "It's for the reinvention we were telling you about," she reminded Treena, "to make Erin perfect for the dog show. And I thought if you shaped her hair — *just a little* — then the henna would work better and —"

"Henna!" Treena and Erin spoke in unison.

Vigorously Cassie nodded her head. "I thought we'd try henna on your hair. I bought it yesterday at the superstore. You can pay me back whenever you want," she added generously. "No rush." She looked particularly pleased with herself.

The kettle began to boil. Treena stood up and started to pour the water through the drip.

Erin leaned back until her chair was touching the wall. How typical of Cassie to make plans without even asking her. "You know, we didn't talk about henna or cutting my hair or anything like that," she said crossly.

"We did, you just don't remember. Anyway, it was all my idea," Cassie bragged. "And you're going to love it, trust me."

Trust me. Those words had gotten her and Cassie into trouble ever since Erin had been coming to Courtenay for the summer. Like the time they had given Cassie's cat, Zeus, a buzz cut. The cat had squirmed, the razor had slipped out of Erin's hand, and the poor animal had ended up looking like something out of a horror movie. It had taken a full year for the fur to grow back, and Zeus still ran away every time Erin even looked at him.

"What's henna anyway?" Erin asked.

"You know. It's that Egyptian plant dye stuff," Cassie said excitedly. "In some parts of the world, they put it on their hands and the bottoms of their feet, too." Her eyes widened. "You know what, we probably have enough to try that, too. We could make a pattern and —"

Erin did know. "The stuff's red. I don't want it on my hands and feet. I'm not sure I want it on my hair, either. Maybe something lighter would —"

"Treena does it all the time," Cassie interrupted, "and her hair's not red."

Treena finished pouring the water and sat back down. Erin stared at the subtle red highlights in her blonde hair. They looked so natural. She'd had no idea Treena used henna. "What if it stings?" she asked Cassie, remembering the disastrous episode with the Wart Away.

"It doesn't sting, does it, Treena?"

Her older sister shook her head. "No, but if Erin doesn't want to, she doesn't want to." She took a bite from the muffin, flipped the paper open to the travel section, and began to read.

Cassie ignored her. "I bought one called Midnight Plum." She stared at Erin's hair. "It's supposed to give you plummy-red highlights. Come on," she encouraged. "It's no big deal. Your hair's so dark probably no one will even notice. Just us. And Treena won't take much off the ends, will you, Treen?"

"Whatever you want, *Erin*." Treena frowned at her sister. "Don't be pushy. It's not your decision."

Cassie leaned close so Treena couldn't hear. "It's going to be a new you, remember?" she whispered in Erin's ear. "For the dog show. For next year." She grinned.

Erin's anger dissolved. Cassie was right. "Just how plummy is Midnight Plum, anyway?" she asked.

Cassie gave a triumphant whoop and Erin grinned. It was going to be a perfectly plummy reinvention.

* * * *

"You want me to put *that* on my hair?" Erin peered at the green mud in the bowl. It looked like mushed cooked peas. Like baby food. She leaned closer and sniffed. "Eww. You've got to be kidding." It smelled like the compost pile her grandmother kept at the end of the garden.

Cassie giggled. "If it was good enough for Cleopatra, it's good enough for you." She picked up a paintbrush and dipped it in the slime. "It's not so bad. You get used to the smell after a while. Treena did."

"I don't know." Erin watched the green goop cling to the end of the brush. She was starting to have second thoughts. "Shouldn't we test it first or something?"

"Why?" Cassie poked the green slime with her fingernail. "Your mom would love this stuff. It's completely natural."

"Lots of things are completely natural but that doesn't mean I want to wear them!" Erin ran a hand through her clean, wet hair. It felt different already; Treena had taken almost two inches off the ends.

Cassie dropped the brush back into the bowl. "Sit down and put this around your neck." She handed Erin a faded pink towel. "I promise, it won't sting!"

Erin sat while Cassie parted her hair with a large, silver clip. Then she began to apply the henna. Plop. Plop. Plop. She could feel the green mud hitting her hair. When Cassie began to rub it in, it felt warm and gritty.

"It feels like meat sauce or something," she complained. "Only it doesn't smell as good."

Cassie's breath tickled Erin's ear when she laughed. "Just think of it as plant sauce." She plopped another brushful of henna onto Erin's head and began to work it in.

"I don't know about this, Cass." Erin was feeling uneasy. "The stuff's falling off." Little green spitballs of hardened henna were hitting her shoulder and dropping into her lap.

"It doesn't stick very well. Especially at first. Treena warned me about that." She pulled back and frowned at Erin. "It's not stinging your head or anything, is it?"

She shook her head. Little green balls went flying.

"Don't shake," Cassie screeched. Furiously her hands massaged Erin's head as she tried to work the henna into her hair. "A couple more minutes and we'll be done." She reached for the brush. "I promise."

It still felt gritty, Erin thought as Cassie applied the last of the henna, but it had taken so long to get it all on, that the green slime had gone from warm to cool. And though the smell made her wrinkle her nose more than once, it didn't sting one bit. It may have felt better than the Wart Away, but it took a whole lot longer to apply. After that, she had to sit with a plastic cover on her hair for an entire hour! She could hardly move. When she did, the henna fell off her head in plops and balls.

Finally, after what seemed like forever, it was time to rinse.

"Bend over more." Cassie pushed Erin's head closer to the kitchen sink.

"Owww!" She tried to lean forward. "I'm bending as much as I can."

"Maybe the bathroom would be easier," Cassie suggested as she turned on the hot water. "It's just that the kitchen sink has this great nozzle that we can move around." She pulled it out for Erin to inspect. "See?"

"This is fine." Erin stood on her toes and leaned as far forward as she could without falling over. "Let's just do it." She couldn't wait to see the color of her hair.

"Tell me how this feels." Cassie brought the nozzle to Erin's scalp.

"Hot!" she yelped.

"Sorry." Cassie adjusted the taps. "How's this?"

"Better."

They had a plan. Cassie directed the water and Erin rubbed at the henna. The plan didn't work. The henna didn't want to come out. It sat there like a green slide as the water ran off.

"Oh, no!" Erin wailed. She could see it now. She'd have little green spitballs in her hair forever. "It has to come out," she said. "It has to."

"Relax. We just need more water pressure. That's all." Cassie adjusted the taps and tried again. It didn't work.

Erin's bad feeling grew bigger. Her hair was going to be green. Gritty, globby green. Forever. "Call Treena," she ordered. "Or your Mom. Call somebody." She could see it now. At the dog show. Going to school. With green hair. And it wasn't even a nice lime green. It was slime green.

"Treena went out," Cassie said nervously. "And Mom's working in the shop. I know, maybe we should fill the bathtub and put you underwater. For sure it'll come out then."

"No!" Sometimes Cassie could be so weird. "Get the directions," Erin instructed. "And read them out loud to me."

Cassie reached for the henna box. "'Work into the hair thoroughly.' We did that."

"Keep going."

"'Leave for an hour.'"

"Uh-huh."

"'After one hour, shampoo hair and rinse thorough-ly,'" Cassie read. "'Follow with conditioner.'" She threw the box down. "I'll get my mom's shampoo and be right back." She ran from the room.

The shampoo and conditioner worked. So did the henna. Her hair was perfect, Erin decided later as she stared at her reflection in her grandmother's hall mirror. Burgundy black. The color of plums. It didn't smell much like plums but she was sure that horrible green plant smell would disappear sooner or later. Besides, nobody was going to be close enough to smell it.

"Grandma," Erin called, walking into the kitchen. She could hardly wait to see if her grandmother noticed the change. "Grandma, are you here?" There was no welcoming answer, no scramble of nails on tile as Blue rushed toward her. The house was silent. Empty.

Erin found them in the kennel. The other dogs howled their indignation as Erin walked by their cages without stopping. Her feet slowed in front of Abby's cage and, after a fast look to make sure her grandmother wasn't looking, Erin quickly tossed a dog biscuit through the bars. The beagle pounced on it like she hadn't eaten in weeks.

"Hello, darlin'." Her grandmother didn't look up as Erin approached. She was on her knees in front of Duchess. Her square, capable hands were skimming the dog's stomach. "How was your afternoon with Cassie?"

"Fine." Blue came to lick her wrist and Erin scratched his head. After nosing at her pocket and finding the other dog biscuit, he wandered back to the corner to lay beside Duchess. "How is she?" Erin asked. The yellow Lab seemed to get bigger every time she saw her.

"All her vitals are good," Grandma said slowly. She was sucking on a candy; Erin could see the small bulge in her cheek. "And the puppies are still moving well. But if I'm not mistaken, she's going to be in labor in the next few days. And it's too soon."

"It's not that early, is it?"

Grandma pushed the candy from one side of her mouth to the other. "It's borderline." Worry made her voice higher than normal. "Dogs usually go into labor anywhere between fifty-nine and sixty-three days. Duchess is at fifty-seven days."

Erin tossed her head again. Her hair bounced softly against her shoulders. "That's close," she said encouragingly. She wished her grandmother would turn around.

"True. But with dogs every day counts." Grandma sighed and stood up. "I'd be happier if she'd wait at least a few more days." She turned and gave Erin a reassuring pat on the arm. "Not to worry, m'darlin'. Nature knows best. These things have a way of working out." She stared at Erin's hair and then smiled. "Very nice." She reached out to touch it. "Who cut it — Cassie?"

"Treena. Do you like the color?" She threw her head back and spread out the ends of her hair with her fingers. She caught another whiff of that plant smell. Oh, well. Suffering through that globby green slime had been worth every second.

"I think it's delightful. You've got just enough red in there to be interesting. What did you use?"

"Henna."

"Turn around," Grandma ordered. She nodded her approval when Erin turned to face her again. "Very sophisticated," she proclaimed. "It makes you look years older."

Erin grinned. Older! She looked older.

Her grandmother slipped an arm around Erin's shoulders, crunched down on her candy, and began to walk. "Come on, Blue," Grandma called. "Time for dinner. The pizza should be here any minute." The only part of Blue that moved was his head as he lifted it to stare after them.

"He's staying," Erin said. "I don't think he wants to leave Duchess."

"Fair enough." Her grandmother leaned so close that Erin could smell the minty sweetness of her breath. "When your parents see your hair, they're going to kill me." She chuckled and gave her a squeeze. "But don't let that bother you, Erin, darlin'. It wouldn't be the first time." She laughed again, then stopped as she caught sight of the pizza delivery man. "Oh, here's supper."

Erin watched her rush ahead to the man who waited impatiently on the steps. So what if Grandma didn't knit and cook like other grandmothers. She raised dogs and ordered pizza instead. And she didn't flip out over a haircut and a henna job. The smell of cheese and pepperoni carried on the wind. Her stomach gave a nasty growl. She began to walk faster. Her grandmother was cool. Cassie had said so herself. She was so cool she would probably let Erin shave her legs. All she had to do was ask!

10

Erin had written Rachel several letters since arriving in Courtenay, and the next afternoon she got her first response. Rachel was having "a howling good time" at camp with the Oresti twins. Whatever that meant, Erin thought with a giggle as she quickly skimmed down the page. "Way cool about the dog show," Rachel wrote. "Just think, if you win and get your picture in the paper, you can have your pick of any guy you want in grade seven."

"I don't want a guy," Erin told Blue as they sprawled out on the grass near the kennel, "I just want a dog." The Lab was panting softly after a long walk down by the creek.

The rest of Rachel's letter talked about camp crafts

(boring), camp food (greasy), camp guys (hot), and ended with a reminder that Ridgeway Elementary rocked and grade seven ruled.

Grade seven was coming up fast. So was the dog show. She scratched Blue's head absently, her eyes fastened firmly on the legs that stretched out of her faded denim shorts. It had been way too hot today to wear jeans.

But that meant her legs were on display for everyone to see. Her baboon legs. Ape legs. Beast legs. The words ran through her head like Blue chasing after his Frisbee. She wanted to be perfect for the show. And for her last year in elementary school. She *had* to shave her legs. She'd ask her grandmother today.

Erin sighed, gave Blue a final pat, and then ran a hand over her knees to her calf. Cassie said under all that hair she had great legs. *Under all that hair.* Erin didn't care if the hair was soft and silky. As far as she was concerned, it was like spikes coming out of her skin. She had to get rid of it.

A family of baby sparrows chattered away noisily in the apple tree as the mother bird returned to the nest with something in her beak. Erin watched Blue raise himself on all fours and go to the base of the tree to inspect. After a minute of tail wagging and staring up into the branches, Blue sniffed the base of the tree until he found a small stick. Grasping it firmly between his teeth, he pranced back to Erin and laid it by her feet. His brown eyes grinned at her.

"Go for it, Blue." She threw the stick and watched the Lab run after it. Instead of returning with his prize, he barked and playfully tossed it into the air.

Rolling onto her stomach, she stared at a tiny ant crawling up a blade of grass and twirled a strand of hair between her fingers. She loved her hair! Now that the green plant smell had gone, she loved it even more. John had agreed with her grandmother. The haircut and henna job made her look older. Much older he had said! She held out her crater claw. The ant traveled over her finger, tickling her wart before making its way toward another blade of grass. She smiled when it disappeared. The warts hadn't disappeared yet, but the bigger one had started to itch. That was a change, and she was changing, too. Once she and Cassie finished the perfect reinvention, she would be a completely all new Erin Morris. Her thoughts wandered to Rachel and the start of school.

She could hear the whispers as she walked into the classroom, her hair looking like polished plums, her feet behaving perfectly. No more tripping over themselves. Her legs, her wonderfully long, smooth legs were bare and she wore only the tiniest, flippiest skirt and blouse. There she is, they would whisper, Erin Morris. She placed first in Senior Novice this summer, you know. With this incredibly gorgeous black Lab called Mr. Lavender Blue. She knows everything there is to know about dogs, did you know that? Is she wearing mascara, do you think? Or were her eyelashes always that long? She's a brain, too, that Erin Morris, did you know? How come she wasn't on the basketball team last year? This year I think she should be captain, don't you?

Blue's cold nose sniffed her thigh and her daydream faded. School was forgotten. She giggled as Blue's rough pink tongue came out and licked her leg. When she shaved her legs she would feel things even more — things like dog kisses and wind currents and grass blades tickling her calves.

All of a sudden, summer seemed so much better and she felt so much more grown up. She would be able to wear that white skirt when she went into the ring with Blue, when she won that first place ribbon. It was all going to be perfect. She was almost perfect!

"Hello, darlin'."

Erin jumped. She had been so involved with her thoughts that she hadn't heard Grandma coming. "You scared me," she said breathlessly, looking up at her grandmother. A worried frown creased the older woman's forehead. Erin scrambled to her feet. "What's wrong?" she asked.

Her grandmother headed for the house. Erin followed. "Duchess's stomach has fallen. Her temperature is going down," Grandma explained. "The puppies will be coming soon. I've got to bring her inside and get her comfortable."

"That's okay, isn't it?" Erin held the back door open for her grandmother. "I mean she's almost at sixty days, right?" She waited until Blue was inside as well before fastening the screen behind them.

"She's at fifty-eight days," Grandma reminded her. "I'd be happier if she waited a few more days before giving birth." She walked down the hall to the den, sank into the overstuffed green chair, wearily rubbed her eyes, and plopped her feet on a nearby crate. The large wooden crate was where Duchess would eventually whelp her puppies. Grandma would be right there with her. After the puppies were born, Grandma would curl up in the armchair and doze, keeping one eye on the new mother and puppies through the first night.

An uneasy feeling overcame Erin as she studied her grandmother's slumped shoulders, the preoccupied look in her eyes. It wasn't the time to ask about shaving her legs. She'd have to wait. "I mean, Duchess is going to be all right, isn't she, Grandma?"

Grandma sighed and offered Erin a slight smile. "I hope so, m'darlin'. Dr. Maartens was here earlier and he said everything looks fine. He'll be on standby in case there's an emergency." She glanced around the small den but her eyes eventually came back to the crate. "In the meantime, we'd better get this place cleaned up and be ready for those pups. I want to bring Duchess into the house as soon as we can."

Erin and Grandma worked for two hours, stopping only once to pop several frozen chicken pies into the oven. Erin tidied the den while her grandmother ran a load of towels through the wash. Erin cleaned the brown heat lamp and adjusted the bulb while Grandma checked on supplies. Sensing that something important was going on, Blue refused to leave Erin's side. Even when she was almost finished and was lining the crate with old towels and a few blankets, the black Lab insisted on being in there with her.

"Out of the way, Blue." Grandma scooted the dog aside as she handed Erin a bottle of bright pink nail polish. "Put this in the corner of the crate, would you darlin'? I've got to make a note of Dr. Maartens's emergency number."

Erin stared at the small bottle. Strawberry Ice it was called. "What's this for?" she asked.

Her grandmother was looking in the phone book. "For the puppies," she said absently. "To mark their toes."

"To mark their toes?" She frowned and put the bottle on the shelf. "Why?" Blue, frustrated at the lack of attention, whined and thrust his wet nose into Erin's free hand. She gave him a scratch behind the ears. "It's okay, Blue," she whispered.

Grandma's finger paused on the page. She scribbled a number on a scrap of paper and tucked it beside the phone. After putting the phone book away, she smiled at the look of confusion on Erin's face. "I always mark the toenail of each pup," she explained. "That's how I can tell which is which. The first one born gets the outside left toe painted, the next gets the second from the outside left painted." Grandma stood, hands on hips, surveying the whelping crate. Satisfied, she smiled. "Sometimes they look so much alike, it's hard to remember who's who." She chuckled.

Excitement stirred in Erin's stomach. She laid the last towel down and came out of the crate. Suddenly the puppies were very real to her. Very real and arriving soon. "Do you think I can watch? I've never seen puppies being born."

Grandma slipped an arm around her shoulder. "We'll have to see how Duchess does. Usually the fewer people in the whelping room, the better." She gave Erin's shoulder a reassuring squeeze. "Mind you, if things go easily and if you're very quiet, maybe you can slip in for a little while and watch. Okay?"

"Okay," Erin agreed with a vigorous nod. Blue whined again and stuck his head between the two women. They both laughed.

"He knows something's up. He can sense it." Grandma leaned down to rub Blue's face. "Don't you, boy?" Blue's tail wagged so hard his back end swayed with the movement. "I think he smells the chicken pies, too."

At the mention of food, Erin's stomach growled. "So do I!" The savory smell of chicken and onions and pastry wafted through the air and Erin was hungry.

Grandma straightened. "Tell you what," she said. "You set the table while I go out to check on Duchess. After we eat, we'll bring her inside and settle her down."

It didn't happen quite that fast. After supper came something Grandma called set-up time. Erin thought it was more like fussing time. Her grandmother wanted to make sure there was enough food ready for breakfast and lunch, too. In spite of Erin's assurances that she really was old enough to find the cereal and cut meat for sandwiches, her grandmother had to make sure everything was just so.

"The leftover pizza is here, darlin'." Peggy pointed to the top shelf in the fridge where the pizza sat on a plate. "There are tins of salmon in the pantry, lots of bread in the freezer, and some chicken salad if you'd prefer that." She gestured to the plastic food saver container on the lower shelf. "And I'll put this last chicken pie down here."

Erin just nodded. Grandmothers could be as weird as parents. Why did Grandma think she was old enough to henna her hair but not old enough to figure out what to eat if she was hungry?

"I could be tied up a long time," Grandma told her again. "If you get lonely, you can always give John a call. His number is on the board beside the phone." She shut the fridge and flicked off the kitchen light. "Mind you, he'll probably be over here first thing in the morning for your training session with Blue."

The dog had been lying quietly on his blanket listening to everything Grandma said but he jumped to attention as soon as his name was called.

"You make it sound like you're going away or something." She followed her grandmother to the back door. Blue trotted happily beside them.

"Whelpings are unpredictable and this is Duchess's first time," Grandma explained. "You stay, Blue." She shooed the black Lab into the hallway and quickly shut the door behind them. "I'll probably be here the whole time but there's always a chance I might have to take Duchess over to the animal hospital. I just want you to be prepared, that's all."

The idea of being alone at her grandmother's house didn't bother Erin at all. Besides, she'd have Blue to keep her company. She could feel the Lab's eyes on her back as she walked down the path through the garden toward the kennel. He barked in protest at being left behind.

"Can't we take him down with us?" Erin asked.

Grandma shook her head. "I don't want him all excited around Duchess. She needs quiet right now."

Instead of the barking that usually broke out when anyone approached the kennel, the other dogs were strangely subdued. It was like they knew that birth was imminent. Even Abby, the noisy beagle, simply lifted her head and wagged her tail when Erin and Grandma walked by.

Duchess was lying in a big, round lump right beside the kennel door. She was very still. Only her brown eyes moved. Slowly and solemnly they blinked.

"She looks uncomfortable," Erin observed.

"I'm sure she is." Grandma opened the door and crouched beside Duchess. "Scared, too, no doubt. It's the first time she's done this, remember?" Gently Grandma rubbed behind the Lab's ears. "There we go, sweetheart, it's going to be all right." Slowly her hands moved over the animal's fur, down her neck, and along her back to her stomach. There was a faraway look in her grandmother's eyes as she waited. "I can feel some tightening." She stood and studied the animal. "Probably should have moved her inside before now," she muttered almost to herself. "Mind you, I was hoping she'd hold off a while, but it looks like the puppies will be coming sooner rather than later." She opened the door to the kennel. "Come on, Duchess. Let's go, girl."

The animal didn't move. She just stared at Erin and Grandma like they were crazy.

"Come on, Duchess, let's go," Erin encouraged.

Large brown eyes blinked their refusal.

They tried everything to get Duchess to stand and move. Nothing worked. "Maybe we should carry her," Erin finally suggested.

Grandma shook her head. "She's too heavy. Besides, it's not a good idea with those puppies she's carrying."

"I think we should bring Blue down here," Erin said suddenly. "Duchess will move if Blue's here."

"I don't know." Grandma looked doubtful. "I don't want her excited."

Erin looked at Duchess and giggled. She *did* feel sorry for the animal but it was almost funny the way the dog refused to even lift her head. "I don't think anything's going to get her really excited, Grandma." She giggled again as those brown eyes blinked mournfully. "But maybe if Blue's here, she'll at least stand up."

Grandma leaned her head to one side and considered Erin's words. Finally she nodded. "Let's give it a try. Run and get Blue."

11

It worked. As soon as Duchess saw Blue, she not only stood but also waddled out the kennel door toward the house like she'd been waiting just for him. A few minutes later, the dog was settled in her crate and Peggy was curled up in the old green armchair beside her, a cup of milky tea in hand and an expectant smile on her face.

Erin, meanwhile, had a problem. A problem named Blue. Blue refused — absolutely — to leave the whelping room.

"Come *on*, Blue," She pulled on the black Lab's collar. "Come *on!*" Blue dug his feet into the old carpet and whined. Duchess, curled up on a blue blanket in a corner of the crate, studied him with her large, brown eyes.

"Why don't you take Blue and go see Cassie? Mrs. Walker told me this morning they're leaving a day early on their camping trip. Something to do with coming back early to take care of a flower order." Grandma sipped her tea. "Nothing's going to happen here for a few hours yet and it'll keep you both busy." Her grandmother's eyes remained on Duchess. "Just remember to be careful. Oh, and you might try that springer John bought you," she added.

Cassie was out buying food for the camping trip. Erin decided to ride back along Dove Creek Road, past the creek and the corn fields toward the banks of Tsolum River.

It was a perfect summer night, she thought happily as the breeze skimmed her face. The sun was still high enough in the sky to warm her shoulders and cast shadows on the road. Blue ran contentedly beside her. Erin smiled as he tried to chase a bird — he couldn't go very far on the springer. When they reached the river, Erin glanced around to make sure they were alone. Satisfied that there was no sign of Mark or Robert, she tossed her bike on the rocks.

"Woof!"

She giggled and released the dog. "Okay, Blue, okay!" She reached for a rock and threw it. Blue dove into the water and searched. He surfaced without it. His face was puzzled. He stared at her as if to ask, "what happened?" Erin laughed out loud. "Relax," she told him. "I'll find another one." She searched the ground for the kind of flat rock that skipped across the water so well. Blue caught the second one and for several minutes the two of them played fetch and toss. After a while, Blue swam out into the river to cool off. She sat down beside her bike and watched him paddle. Soon he disappeared behind a large rock.

"Look, Bro', we have company!"

Erin jumped. It didn't sound like Mark or Robert. She turned her head and looked. It wasn't.

Two older boys smirked at her. One was tall and thin and had a cigarette dangling from his lips. The shorter one had stringy black hair and carried a boom box. "Wanna join our party?"

"No, thanks," Erin stood up and faced them. Her palms were sweaty; she wiped them on her shorts.

"Why not?" asked the tall one. He pulled the cigarette from his lips and flicked the ashes to the ground.

She didn't answer. These two made Mark and Robert look like a couple of preschoolers. In spite of the warm night, she suddenly had goose bumps on her arm. Briskly she rubbed at them.

"She's got places to go, don't you, sister?" The kid with the boom box kicked her bike. "Nice machine."

"I could use a bike." The tall kid's eyes narrowed as he stared at her. "How much you want for it?"

She swallowed. "It's not for sale." *Hurry up, Blue,* she chanted to herself. *We need to get out of here. These guys are dangerous.*

"Well, then, I guess I'll just have to help myself." His smirk widened to show crooked front teeth. "Kind of like a present from you to me."

The hot, sour taste of fear scalded the back of her throat and rendered her momentarily speechless. With a bravery she didn't feel, she grabbed her bike and faced the two boys. "I said it's not for sale," she said again when her voice returned. Her hands were shaking and she clutched the handlebars. All she had to do was wheel toward the river, find Blue, and get out. Blue. His springer. The harness. She reached for them. As she did, the kid with the boom box yanked the bike away from her.

"Hey!" she yelled. "Give it back!"

High-pitched laughter was their only response. "In your dreams, sister. In your dreams," said the tall, skinny kid. He laughed again.

Just then Blue shot out of the water and came running. The sight of him gave her the necessary courage to reach out and grab the bike back. "It's mine," she yelled loudly. "Now get lost."

Blue raced to her side, dropped the stick from his mouth, and bared his teeth at the two boys. The hair on the back of his neck stood up like black toothpicks. His tail was down between his back legs. Water made him shiny and slick. There was a deep, fierce growl coming from the back of his throat. *Grrrrrr.* He stepped a bit closer to the boys.

"Hey, man." The kid with the boom box held up his free hand and kept his eyes fastened on Blue. "We were only kidding, man." He laughed nervously.

"Ya," The tall, skinny kid flicked his cigarette to the ground and slowly backed up. "Call your dog off, okay?" He fidgeted with his watchstrap.

"I can't call him off," Erin lied. "He's an attack dog. If you're not out of here in two minutes flat, he'll jump you and go for your neck! You'd better get lost."

"We're going." Both boys backed up. Their eyes were big and round and glued to Blue. "Just keep him back, okay?"

Erin's knees were shaking now, too. She held the bike for support and stared the two boys down. "Just go," she said. "And fast."

Blue growled again and the two boys turned and ran. Blue took two steps forward and barked.

"It's okay Blue," Erin whispered as she watched the boys scramble over the rocks and disappear into the trees. "They're gone now." She kneeled down and put her arms around the Lab's neck. He was dripping wet but she didn't care. "Good boy!" she said. She scratched his ears and rubbed the top of his head. "Good, good boy!" She leaned her forehead against his. His tail lifted and began to sway. Slowly the toothpicks on his neck disappeared. He nudged Erin's hand, wanting more. When he saw the harness on the ground he pulled away and barked. A happy bark this time. A "let's go" bark.

"You may be ready but I'm not." She scanned the river for a sign of the boys. Nothing. "I need to stop shaking first." She took a couple of deep, steadying breaths. In all the years she'd come to the banks of the Tsolum River, nothing like this had ever happened before. She was going to have to be more careful. And be careful to always bring Blue with her.

She fastened Blue to the springer and began rolling the bike over the rocks. Normally she would let the Lab run ahead, but not tonight. Tonight she wanted him as close to her side as possible.

The ride home was uneventful. By the time Erin and Blue turned into the driveway and strolled past the dented mailbox and the bushy holly tree, she had stopped shaking and Blue was almost completely dry. With the sun setting in pink streaks between the blackened silhouettes of the fir trees and the night sounds of the crickets filling the air, she was feeling almost normal again.

Blue drank long and hard from his yellow bowl before settling on his blanket by the stove. Erin gulped some lemonade before hurrying down the hall to Duchess and Grandma. Wait till Grandma heard how Blue had saved the day!

Her grandmother was crouched inside the crate. If she heard the door open, she paid no attention. Erin held her breath and tiptoed around the crate until she could see Duchess and her grandmother.

There was a puppy! A small tan bundle all slick and shiny with the signs of birth. Thoughts of the boys by the river disappeared. Her heart began to pound. Her breath caught in a whistle between her teeth. It looked like a dog but it didn't. Its eyes were shut and its whole body was curled around itself like those hermit crabs she sometimes found hiding under the rocks at the beach.

Grandma glanced up. "You're just in time," she whispered with a smile. "Puppy number one." After Duchess finished licking the puppy clean, Grandma gently pried open its mouth and checked the airway for mucus. Legs stretched, a tail unfurled. The puppy began to look more normal. Satisfied, Peggy cradled the small animal in her arms. "Hand me the nail polish, would you, darlin'? I've got to keep track, you know."

Duchess seemed oblivious to her presence, so Erin sat quietly on the old green chair. It seemed to take forever for the next puppy to be born. Duchess moved restlessly around the crate, peering toward her behind occasionally as though she didn't understand what was happening. After a while, she began to whine. Then she stood still. Even from several feet away, Erin could see the muscles in Duchess's stomach squeeze and pull. Contractions, Grandma called them. The dog's whining got louder, deeper. Finally, after whipping her tail and hunching her back a few times like she was a camel, Duchess gave a long, deep moan. A bubble appeared. It grew bigger and then it slithered out, carrying puppy number two. It was shiny black and perfectly quiet and still.

Roughly, Duchess nudged the amniotic sac and then tore at it with her teeth. Erin's heart lurched. Was something wrong? A puppy tumbled out in a gush of fluid, squirming and beginning to whimper as Duchess licked and cleaned and stimulated it to life.

Erin began to breathe again. After a few minutes of attention, Duchess turned away and Grandma took over. Once the newborn was checked, Grandma held the bundle out. "It's a little boy," she said with a smile.

Erin's stomach flipped. She wasn't sure she wanted to touch it! Not yet. "I . . . I can't . . ."

"Of course, you can," Grandma insisted softly.

"Take him and mark his toe. Second one from the left on his right foot," she instructed.

Gingerly, using both hands, she accepted the tiny black puppy. Her grandmother was confident enough to hold him in the palm of her hand but Erin was too nervous for that. She could feel his heart beating beneath her fingers. She stared down at him, in awe of a new life that only minutes before hadn't been.

His eyes were so tightly shut they looked like someone had sewn them closed. And though his fur was softer than Erin's white angora sweater, he wasn't nearly as pretty close up. His face was scrunched and red and his nose looked mottled and too big for his face. His arms and legs were too long for his body and they were moving and stretching like limp strands of spaghetti hanging from a fork. He was altogether ugly. Helplessly, hopelessly ugly. And Erin loved him! Gumby. That's what she would call him. If he was hers to call.

"Hello, Gumby," she whispered, searching for the tiny toenail hidden in the fur. Satisfied that she'd found the right one, she carefully dabbed on bright pink Strawberry Ice nail polish. It glittered like a tiny pink ring in the black fur. Reluctant to hand Gumby back to her grandmother, she held him against her chest and gently touched her nose to the top of his soft head. He smelled like pure puppy. Her heart melted.

Her parents just *had* to let her have a puppy of her own. After this summer, they just had to!

When Grandma looked up, her eyes narrowed slightly at the sight of little Gumby tucked under her chin. "Someday," she said softly, guessing what thoughts were going through Erin's mind. "Someday you'll have a dog of your own to love."

It was almost midnight by the time Erin went to bed. Two more puppies had been born — both yellow — and Erin had dutifully marked their toenails with Strawberry Ice. As sweet as the animals were, none evoked the feelings she had for Gumby, the only black Lab of the litter so far. Grandma promised Erin there'd be several more puppies for her to greet in the morning and, as she dragged herself down the hall to bed, she hoped there would be at least one more black Labrador in the bunch.

* * * *

There were, as it turned out the next morning, two more black Labrador puppies. Erin rubbed the sleep from her eyes and stared at them. Six puppies in all — three black and three yellow. All were nursing eagerly from Duchess, who was lying on her side with resigned acceptance. Erin searched for Gumby but it was almost impossible to tell the puppies apart. Her grandmother had been right. Marking their toes with nail polish had been a good idea. One of the black puppies, however, looked larger than the others. Erin wondered if that was Gumby. Beside her, Blue gave out something that sounded like a cross between a whine and a howl.

"Ssssh!" She scolded. Nervously she peered down the hall. There was no sign of her grandmother. Maybe she had decided to sleep in her own bed, after all. "Be quiet," she ordered sternly. "You're not supposed to be in here. But just because you're a hero, I've broken the rules a bit." Blue whined his protest. Duchess thumped her tail against the newspaper. She seemed unconcerned by their presence but Erin knew her grandmother would have her head if she caught Blue in here disturbing the pups. Especially while they were nursing.

The back door slammed. She heard footsteps. Her grandmother! "Come on!" Hero or not, he had to go. She grabbed Blue's collar. He dug in his heels. She pulled. He whined one more time, flopped on his belly, put his head on his front paws, and stared at Duchess and her babies.

"Hello, darlin'." Her grandmother's smile was bright but her face looked pale and tired. "You must have just gotten up. I've only been outside a few minutes." Grandma stopped in the doorway when she caught sight of Blue. "Blue!" She put her hands on her hips. "We have a rule. No other dogs in this room."

Blue's eyes acknowledged Grandma with a blink before flicking back to Duchess and the pups. He whined again and edged forward so his black nose was touching the bottom of the crate.

Grandma sighed. "All right, Blue, you can have a few minutes. But that's it." She joined Erin and dropped a loose arm around her shoulder. "Sleep well?" she asked before turning her attention to the dogs in the crate.

Erin nodded. Except for a dream about two headless

boys who'd come tearing out of the river on huge camels, she'd slept fine. But telling her grandmother about the nightmare would take too much explaining, so she was silent. She was too interested in Duchess and her babies. Several of the puppies were finished nursing now, and Duchess was starting to clean them. Slowly and methodically her pink tongue licked their fur, gently rolling them from side to side. "It's hard to believe they grow up so quickly," she said. "When will they start to walk?"

"It won't be long. They start wobbling around even before their eyes open. At least they should." She hesitated. "I'm not sure about one of the black ones, though." Grandma chewed the corner of her lower lip.

"Why?"

"He has a problem with his left rear leg," Grandma explained. "It's twisted around in a strange way." She glanced at her watch. "I'm going to call Dr. Maartens this morning. It could be a clubfoot. I'm not sure."

"What does that mean?"

Her grandmother hesitated. "It's not good, Erin. If it rights itself, it's fine . . . but if not . . ." Her voice trailed away.

All of a sudden, Erin's mouth was very dry. She swallowed. Not Gumby! It couldn't be Gumby. "Which one is it?" she asked breathlessly. "Was it the one I marked?"

"No." Her grandmother shook her head. "It was the last one born. Perhaps he was squished during the pregnancy."

She tasted sweet relief. "Thank goodness," she

breathed.

"Thank goodness?" Her grandmother arched her eyebrows. For once she seemed to completely misunderstand Erin. "I hardly think it's anything to be thankful for," she said tartly.

She flushed. "No . . . I mean . . . I thought . . ."

Grandma's face softened and she gave her shoulders a squeeze. "I know, darlin'. I know what you meant. I'm just tired and feeling crabby. I hate getting a puppy that's not right." She propelled Erin toward the door. "It's happened twice before and I should be used to it, but it never gets any easier. Come on, Blue!" Grandma's voice sounded funny. Too high or something. "Time for breakfast." She started down the hall.

"What will you do, Grandma?"

Her grandmother was silent. She continued to walk.

"Grandma?" Erin asked again. "What will you do?"

Grandma stopped in the doorway of the kitchen and stared straight ahead. She picked at a button on her blouse and avoided Erin's eyes. "We'll see what the vet says, darlin'. Maybe I made a mistake. Maybe the leg will right itself in a day or two. If not, we can always try a brace. See if that helps."

"And if it doesn't?"

Grandma's eyes, when she finally did look at her, were shiny bright. "If it doesn't, we'll have to put him down. It's the only way," she said softly. "He'll have no quality of life, Erin, m'darlin'. None at all."

12

"So then the vet came and insisted on putting the puppy to sleep," Erin told Cassie as the two girls sat on the floor in Cassie's bedroom, "but Grandma said no." Cassie had just come back from her camping trip with her family and Erin was filling her in on everything that had happened during the week she was away. Between the birth of the puppies and the training sessions with Blue, the days had gone quickly but Erin had still been anxious for Cassie to come home.

"I wanted to try the brace and Grandma agreed even though Dr. Maartens said it was hopeless. He told Grandma to call when . . ." Erin lowered her voice, "when she was ready to take care of things." The words made her stomach flip all over again. "I'm exercising him every single day until he learns to walk." She stopped. "I'm calling him Twister," she whispered.

"Cool name."

"I thought so." The afternoon was hot and muggy; even with the window wide open there was barely any breeze. Clouds the color of wet sand were filling the sky. The birds were silent; the bees were still. The weatherman was calling for a storm, which suited Erin's mood perfectly. Poor Twister. Barely a week old. So far the exercises weren't helping much.

Cassie reached into the bowl of popcorn on the floor between them. "We had to put an animal down once." She crunched on a kernel. "When a foal was born with its kidneys outside its body. My dad and Dr. Maartens took him into the field and shot him," Unconcerned, Cassie licked her fingers. "But they didn't wait. They did it right away."

Erin gasped.

"It's for the best, really it is," Cassie added quickly when she saw the look of horror on Erin's face. "That horse should have been born dead. And those exercises may not work for Twister." She grabbed another handful of popcorn. "It would have been easier to do it right away, like the vet said. For sure before you named him."

Erin shrugged. "Maybe." The exercises would work! They had to work! Rather than asking Grandma if she could adopt Gumby, Erin had decided that Twister was the animal for her. She could give him the love he needed. *She* could help him learn to walk.

Erin scratched Blue's head. His eyes were moving back and forth from Cassie to the popcorn bowl like a Ping-Pong ball. The black Lab had come with her to Cassie's house. After her grandmother had heard about the incident at the river, she was more than willing to let Blue go anywhere with her. "My mom believes there's a reason for everything," she told Cassie. "Pain and illness even."

Cassie pulled on her ear cuff. "Ya, and hair on your legs, too, right?"

In spite of her sadness, Erin grinned. "That too!"

"Did you ask your grandma about shaving them?"

She shook her head. She hadn't thought about her legs very much since Twister had been born. "We've both been too busy."

"The show's less than two weeks away," Cassie pointed out. "You have to shave them. You just have to."

"I don't know." Why had she come to Cassie's anyway? Erin wondered. While her friend had been camping, she'd longed for her to come back so they could talk. Now she didn't feel like visiting. All she could think about was poor little Twister. And helping the dog learn to walk.

Exasperated, Cassie pushed the popcorn bowl aside, jumped up, and grabbed a large purple hand mirror from under the pile of debris on her desk. She thrust the mirror under Erin's nose. "Look. Just look. Your hair is great, your eyebrows have just the right arch. You're almost there. You're almost perfect. Just a few more touches and the reinvention will be finished. Just in time to take Blue into the ring."

"Maybe."

Cassie sat down on the edge of the bed with a loud sigh. "You've been a grump since you got here," she complained.

"I'm worried about Twister." She refused to look at her friend. Instead she stared at one of the horse posters Cassie had taped to her wall. "It's just not fair!"

"It wasn't fair that the foal had to die, either." Tossing the mirror aside, Cassie slid from the bed to the floor and nudged Erin with her toe. "Come on, my dad's in the business of horses and your grandma's in the business of dogs. We have to breed the best horses we can, and your grandma has to breed the best dogs she can. It makes sense when you think about it."

"It doesn't seem very nice though. I think your mom has the right idea. Raise flowers instead."

"Yeah, but if they die she moans and groans like she's lost an animal or something." Cassie smiled but when Erin didn't respond with a smile of her own, she turned serious again. "Look, your grandma's trying the brace. Maybe that'll help. And I could be wrong about the exercises. Maybe they'll work, too. Besides, five of the puppies are healthy. One isn't. Just don't think about the one that isn't." She picked up the popcorn and shoved it under Erin's nose. "Now eat!" she said bossily. "And let's talk about the reinvention."

Blue whined and smacked the bowl with his right paw. Both girls giggled.

"Okay, Blue. Catch." Erin tossed a kernel into the air and Blue caught it before it hit the ground. Cassie was right. Her grandma was trying the brace. She was doing the exercises. Why should she worry? Besides, she had a dog show to worry about instead.

"You have new hair," Cassie continued. "And new eyebrows. Not only that, I'm sure the spell's starting to work because your warts are starting to shrivel. I bet the garlic is rotting in the ground as we speak."

Erin studied her hand. The warts did seem a little bit smaller. Especially the older, larger one.

"All that's left of the perfect reinvention is your legs," Cassie said. "Unless you want to leave them as they are?"

Erin's hair swung forward as she dipped into the popcorn bowl. She had to look her best. Sheila Jones had said so and she should know. She had been a judge once. Erin had to do something about her legs. "Instead of shaving, what about that special cream you were talking about?" she asked, stuffing a handful of popcorn into her mouth.

Cassie let out a hoot of excitement. The popcorn went flying to the floor and Blue scrambled to clean up. "Yes!" she said triumphantly.

* * * *

"I don't know about this, Cassie. It just doesn't feel right." Erin was balanced on the bathroom vanity, wedged between the sink and the door, with her foot propped up on the edge of Cassie's bathtub. She peered at her right leg. All she could see was foam. Gobs and gobs of white foam. She couldn't decide if it smelled more like rubber boots or a really stinky perfume. It just smelled awful. And it felt a whole lot worse. "It's burning my leg," she said nervously. "Like acid or something."

"Whoever said being beautiful was easy?" Cassie asked brightly. She was perched on the toilet painting her toenails with polish called Hot Cocoa. Blue was crammed against the bathtub, his brown eyes fastened firmly on Erin.

"It just doesn't feel right." She jumped down from the vanity, suddenly sure that she didn't want this white goop on her leg anymore. "I want to wash it off. Right now." Blue nudged her leg with his cold nose. A streak of the cream covered his head. "No, Blue!" She wiped the cream from his fur. The sting on her leg was getting worse.

"But we read the directions. And it said we have to keep it on for fifteen minutes." Cassie glanced at the red timer ticking away on the counter. "We still have six minutes to go."

"It also said to test it on your skin first, remember?" Erin reminded her friend. "In case you're allergic or something." Her leg was burning up. It felt like it was on fire. "I think I'm allergic, Cassie. I'm allergic to dust. I'm probably allergic to this hair remover stuff, too." Now it was starting to itch. A hot, burning itch that was worse than anything she'd ever felt in her life. "Run the water, Cassie. I'm taking this stuff off right now!"

Blue stood up and began to whine.

"Now!"

Cassie jumped up. Her nail polish fell to the floor

and Hot Cocoa dribbled out. "Oh, no!" she cried, staring at the mess. "Mom's going to kill me."

"Never mind!" Erin cried back. "We'll clean it up later. Just turn on the water." Blue whined and tried to wrap himself around Erin's leg, covering one side of his fur with the white leg cream as he went.

"Hurry up," Erin said nervously. "Now it's on Blue. We have to rinse him off, too." She could feel tears gathering behind her eyes.

Cassie turned on the tap. Erin stuck her leg under the stream of water and scrubbed furiously with the brown washcloth Cassie handed her. Slowly, the water dissolved the foam and eased the itch, but her leg still burned. "Get Blue in the tub, Cass. We have to clean him off."

"I can't do that! I'm already going to be in trouble for this!" Cassie was wiping up the nail polish on the floor.

"Well, that's nothing compared to the trouble I'll be in if Blue goes bald!" Erin blinked hard to stop the tears from falling. "Grandma will kill me. And I can't take a bald dog into the ring. We have to get him washed!"

Cassie agreed and the two girls hoisted the animal into the tub. Blue thought it was a game. He stood still while they cleaned him off but then he started to jump and prance and play with the brown loofah hanging from the shower shelf. Cassie forgot her fears and thought it was all very funny. Erin didn't.

Her leg was still burning up. She was scared to look at it. What if she'd wrecked it forever? What if she'd permanently damaged her skin? Cassie had promised her the cream was safe. Maybe she was just having an allergic reaction. Blue shook and droplets of water landed in Erin's eyes. Cassie giggled again but Erin failed to see the humor in the situation. "I'm getting him out now," she told Cassie. "Do you have a towel I can use to dry him off?"

"I'll dry him," Cassie said. "You sit and put a cold cloth on your leg."

Propping her foot on the counter, Erin watched Cassie dry Blue with an oversized beach towel. Blue lapped up the attention. He even kissed Cassie on the cheek. *Dear God of Dogdom*, Erin said silently, *don't let him go bald*.

"There," Cassie said as she gave Blue one last rub, "as good as new." She threw the towel into the hamper and was about to let Blue out of the bathroom when her eyes landed on the bathtub. "Look," she said, pointing to the bottom of the tub. "It started to work." She reached over and shut off the tap. Blue rested his head on the edge of the tub and wagged his tail.

Erin's eyes followed Cassie's finger. Traces of foamy white cream flecked with black floated toward the drain. The cream had worked!

Taking a long, deep breath, Erin lifted the cloth on her leg. For a minute nothing made sense. But when she realized what she was looking at, she felt sick to her stomach. "Oh, no!" The cream had taken away patches of hair, leaving the rest looking like twisted mini pretzels. What was she going to do?

Cassie studied Erin's leg thoughtfully. "It looks like

a chess board," she finally said. "With those patches of white skin and the dark hair that's left. Very punkish. Somebody would probably pay to have that done." She grabbed some paper towels from under the sink and finished cleaning up the spilled nail polish.

"We have to do something!" Grandma was going to have a fit when she saw her leg. "I can't walk around like this."

"You could just wear jeans." Cassie threw the soiled towels in the trash. "Like you've been doing."

"But I look like a freak. Besides, there's the dog show." At that thought, the tears spilled over. "And Grandma wants me to wear my white skirt."

There was a loud tap on the bathroom door. "You girls all right in there?" It was Cassie's mother.

"Fine!" Cassie yelled back.

Blue woofed twice.

Erin wiped her tears away. "We're not fine," she hissed. "At least I'm not."

"I know, I know." Cassie looked worried, too. "We'll have to shave the rest off." She handed Erin her jeans. "It's the only choice."

"No," Erin shook her head. "I'm in enough trouble already. If I shave my legs, Mom'll kill me.

Cassie was quiet for a minute. Then she said, "Get dressed. I have a plan."

"What now?"

"You'll see." Cassie pulled open the top drawer of the vanity and began to search for something. "I've got the perfect solution."

"I've heard that before," Erin muttered.

But Cassie was too busy searching through one of the drawers in the vanity to answer.

* * * *

"Owww!" Erin screeched. Her eyes were watering from the pain. "That hurt!" She leaned against the wall and stared miserably around Cassie's bedroom. This was a dumb idea. A really, really dumb idea.

"Try the ice cube again," Cassie told her. "And keep still. You're wiggling around too much." She held the tweezers up triumphantly before she laid another twisted black hair on the paper towel beside Erin. "Got another one!" she said.

"You'd be wiggling around too if someone was plucking the hair on your legs with a pair of tweezers." Erin pressed her back into the wall in preparation for the next round. "This is going to take forever," she moaned as she felt another twinge.

"Anything for beauty I always say." Cassie kept plucking.

Erin's leg was hot and prickly. It hurt even more than the time she had stepped on the bee's nest and ended up with five stings up the back of her leg. "I think we should stop, Cass." She forced herself to look at her leg again. It was still covered with blotches of white skin and black hair but now there were red welts, too. "I think I'm having a reaction to that cream," she said uneasily.

"That's just from plucking," Cassie reassured her. "Trust me. It happens all the time." Her hands moved to another spot on Erin's leg. "You should have seen my eyebrows when Treena plucked them. They were red for over an hour."

Erin sighed and glanced at the clock radio beside Cassie's bed. "Five more minutes then," she told her friend. "And then we're stopping no matter what."

It took fifteen minutes for Erin to convince Cassie to stop. By then it was obvious that the red blotches weren't just from the tweezers. Her entire leg was blotchy. "I *am* having a reaction to that cream!" She held another wet washcloth against her leg. "Now what am I going to do?"

Cassie was sitting on the bed beside her. "I never thought it would do that." Her forehead creased into a nervous frown. "I'm really sorry, Erin. Really I am. My mom uses the stuff all the time and she never has any problems."

"Well, I'm not your mother," Erin muttered. But then she felt bad. She really shouldn't be mad at Cassie. Her friend was only trying to help. She moved the washcloth to another spot on her leg. The cool water was soothing.

There was a whimper from the corner of the bedroom. Blue was dreaming. Erin watched the dog's ears twitch and his eyelids move. He whined again. Erin had a sudden vision of a bald Blue or worse, a half-bald Blue with tufts of twisted pretzel hair where his fur used to be. "Oh man," she breathed. "If that cream did this to me, Blue could be in real trouble."

A look of horror crossed Cassie's face. Obviously, she hadn't thought of that. "I'll call Treena." She jumped off the bed and raced to the door. "She'll know what to do."

"No!" Erin shook her head. The last thing she wanted was Treena the glamor queen in the bedroom laughing at her. She might tell Chad, her unboyfriend, who might tell Mark and Robert. "I'll figure it out myself!" She crumbled the washcloth into a ball and put it on the bedside table.

Cassie sat down on the edge of the bed and stared first at Erin's leg and then at Blue. "Your grandma will know what to do," she said finally, in her quiet, "I think I'm in trouble now" voice.

"I don't know." How could she tell her grandmother? Grandma thought she was responsible enough to take Blue into the show ring. And responsible enough to look after him well the rest of the time. She wouldn't be impressed when she found out the dog had been smeared with hair removal cream. Erin's stomach flipped over. She wouldn't be impressed if Blue went bald, either. "I guess I'm going to have to tell her," she said in a small voice.

"I'll come with you," Cassie offered bravely.

Erin shook her head. "No, I'll do it myself."

"Are you sure?" she asked.

"I'm sure," Erin said. She glanced nervously at the spot on Blue's side. It looked normal. So far. The dog was still dreaming. His legs and ears were twitching. "It'll be better if I do this myself."

"Really?" Cassie looked relieved.

She *did* want Cassie to come, but her parents were always talking about being responsible for your actions. Erin figured this was one of those times she had to be responsible, no matter how much trouble she got in. "I'll do it myself." Her mouth stung like bitter lemon. It was the taste of worry. She swallowed, hoping to chase it away. "It'll be fine," she said firmly. It *had* to be fine.

13

"Have another piece of chicken, darlin'." Grandma held the platter under Erin's nose. Blue, lying quietly on his bed, followed the platter of chicken with his eyes.

Politely, Erin shook her head. She shifted her legs again and tried to resist the urge to scratch. She lost. For the one hundredth time since she had sat down to dinner, her fingers reached under the table to her leg. Scratch, scratch, scratch. It was the absolute worst itch she'd ever had. What *was* she going to do? Nervously she studied Blue. So far the dog had all his fur. So far.

Grandma helped herself to a chicken leg and put the platter down. "I'm still not sure what to do about that pup." She spooned carrots out of the bowl and placed them beside the chicken. "Dr. Maartens was here again. He thinks it's time."

Erin's fingers stopped mid-scratch. Not yet! Twister would be fine. She would exercise him until he walked! Until he ran.

Grandma sighed and stared blankly at the food on her plate. "I'm just not sure," she said again.

Erin had been sure when she'd come home from Cassie's house that her grandmother would know something was wrong. But Grandma hadn't noticed her mad rush into the bedroom to grab some jeans, nor had she said anything about her continual scratching. It was because her grandmother was worried about Twister.

"What about the brace?" Erin's leg was itchy again. This time she wouldn't scratch. She *wouldn't*.

"Dr. Maartens says it's not working," Grandma said softly as she pushed her chicken leg around the plate. "It could take some time and with the way the other dogs are picking on him . . ."

"Picking on him? On Twister?" All of a sudden Erin was ashamed of herself. Her problem seemed small compared to what Twister was facing.

"Twister?"

Erin flushed. "That's what I've been calling him."

"Don't name him, darlin'." Grandma's eyes were gentle. "Not this one."

Of course, he needed a name. All dogs needed a name. Unless . . . Erin swallowed the lump in her throat. "What do you mean they're picking on him?" She wouldn't think about the "unless" part.

"It happens, Erin. It's survival of the fittest. All animals do it. It usually happens to the smallest one. In this case, it's the one with the bad leg."

"Maybe you should take him out of the litter then." She rubbed at her leg. Rubbing didn't count. It wasn't scratching.

"He needs his mother for another week at least," Grandma explained. "I guess I could isolate him and take him in for feedings, but I don't feel right about it. The poor thing is so listless and sad. He just lies in the corner. He doesn't seem to want to live. Maybe Dr. Maartens is right," she mused. "Maybe it's time to make a decision."

"Wait a few more days." Erin's fingers slipped to her jeans again. Scratch. Scratch. Scratch. "I'm doing these exercises with him and I know they're going to work. He's going to make someone a perfect pet!" Like me, Erin added silently.

"We'll see." Grandma pushed her uneaten chicken away and methodically wiped her fingers on a napkin. "Now," she said, her brown eyes fastened firmly on Erin's face, "just what is the problem with your leg, m'darlin'?"

Erin could feel the flush start at her neck and travel right up past her forehead to the roots of her hair. "What makes you . . . ?" She stopped and dropped her eyes to the table. "I don't have . . ." She stopped again. She'd never lied to her grandmother. And she couldn't do it now. She'd tell the truth and take the consequences.

There was an easy smile on her grandmother's face.

"Just what trouble did you and Cassie concoct this time?"

"I have this rash," she began cautiously, "on my leg."

"And how did that come about?"

"Oh, Grandma, it's just awful," Erin fought to keep back the tears. "Mom won't let me shave my legs but the hair on my legs keeps growing and growing and the kids at school won't shut up about it and now I have to wear a skirt in the ring with Blue so Cassie and I decided to do this reinvention to make me look better and we used this cream but I think I had an allergic reaction and now I'm covered with horrible red marks." The words poured out of Erin. "And when we were washing it off Blue brushed up against my leg and smeared the cream all over his fur so now I'm afraid he'll be bald which would be horrible for a dog and especially one in a dog show!" Erin was out of breath by the time she finished speaking.

"I see." A small smile hovered on her grandmother's lips. "So you used a depilatory."

Erin frowned. "I think that's what it was called."

"And how long did Blue have the depilatory on?"

"Not long. Less than a minute. Way less. We washed it off right away."

Grandma's smile deepened. "He'll be fine, Erin. He has a thick coat. It probably didn't touch the roots. Don't worry about him."

In spite of her grandmother's reassurance, Erin's eyes sought out the spot on Blue's side. It looked perfectly, wonderfully, normal. If only it stayed that way.

"What about you?" Grandma asked. "Did you test the cream on your skin first?"

"No," Erin wailed. "And I told Cassie we should have but you know what Cassie is like . . ."

Grandma pushed her chair back from the table. "Let's see the leg," she said briskly.

Erin spun around, raised her leg, and rested her ankle on her grandmother's knee. Blue, sensing that dinner was over, inched his way forward toward the table, his ears at attention, his eyes focused on the few pieces of chicken remaining on the platter.

"Blanket, Blue," Grandma ordered without even looking up. Gently her fingers went to work rolling up the leg of Erin's jeans.

Her skin was a patchwork of curled black hair and big red welts. Just looking at it made Erin feel sick to her stomach all over again.

Softly her grandmother ran two fingers over her leg. "That's quite the reaction," she murmured. "If it's any consolation at all, my dear, you come by it honestly." She raised her head and gave Erin a sympathetic smile.

"I do?"

"Mm-hmm." Her grandmother nodded before looking back at the leg. "Had the same reaction myself, only I did a skin test on my wrist first. Broke out in horrible welts. Never went near the stuff again."

"What did you do?" Erin demanded again. "What can I do?" She reached over to scratch but her grandmother stopped her.

"Leave it be," she ordered mildly. "Don't aggravate it any more than it already is." She pulled Erin's jeans back into place and lowered her leg to the floor. "A good long soak in Epsom salts will relieve the itch," Grandma said as she stood up. "The redness will take a few days to go, I'll wager. But the show's still a week from Sunday. You'll be fine by then."

"I'll still have hairy legs." A lone tear snaked its way down her cheek. "*Mutated* hairy legs." Another tear escaped and Erin wiped at her face with the back of her hand.

Grandma sat back down. "Why won't your mom let you shave your legs?" she asked softly.

Erin shrugged. "You know Mom. She believes in being as natural as possible. She also thinks I'm too young to decide. She says maybe when I grow hair under my arms then I can shave the hair on my legs."

Grandma snorted indignantly and the sound made Erin giggle through her tears. "That sounds all well and fine but your mother isn't the one going to school every day, is she?" She handed Erin a tissue.

"No." Erin wiped her eyes.

"Have you told your mother what the other kids are saying?"

"No." She blew her nose. "Mom wouldn't understand. The hair on her legs is so blonde you can hardly see it, you know?"

"Oh, I know." Grandma replied.

Erin looked closely at her grandmother. "You know?"

"The kids teased me, too. All the time. And in those days, girls didn't wear pants to school."

"What did you do?"

"Suffer mostly," her grandmother replied. "Wear

thick tights and fight with my mother about shaving my legs." She chuckled. "They didn't have depilatories in those days, either, so I mixed sugar and water to a paste and pulled the hair off. It was torture and my mother and father were furious but it was worth it." She chuckled again. "I was pretty near your age, too."

Hope spread through Erin like a shaft of sunlight entering a darkened room. Her grandmother understood. She really did. "Oh, Grandma, please! Let me shave my legs," Erin begged. "Please!"

Grandma sighed. "I can't say yes. Not when I know your mom has said no." She stopped and studied Erin's face. "Maybe we should talk to her again."

"I've talked to her a bunch of times," Erin said. "And she always says the same old thing. That I'm too young. That it'll grow in thicker. That she loves me warts and all." Automatically Erin's fingers sought out the warts on her left hand. Cassie was right. They *were* getting smaller. At least something was going her way.

"I'll tell her about the trouble you're having." Grandma stood and pulled Erin to her feet. "In the meantime, into the bath with you."

"It would be wonderful if she said yes," Erin babbled happily as she followed her grandmother down the hall. "No more hair on my legs for school next year. It'll be a whole new, perfect me."

"You're perfect now, Erin," her grandmother said as she pulled a bag of Epsom salts from the hall cupboard. "Shaving your legs will change things less than you think."

* * * *

Erin was usually slow to wake up in the morning. Gradually the sound of birdsong would filter through her brain. Gradually she would be aware of Blue wheezing softly on his pillow beside the bed. Then she would stretch and think about breakfast, about what she had planned for the day.

Wednesday she was instantly awake.

Something was different.

Blue was on his pillow, wheezing softly. And he had all his hair, so it wasn't that.

Erin stretched and tried to remember what was different. Then she knew. Her legs were different. They were smooth and slick. Erin rubbed them together a second time. Slip, slide. She grinned. They felt like hot dogs . . . or smooth strands of soft, red licorice.

Grandma had finally gotten through to her mom. Erin's dad had gone to Whistler for a job interview and her mother had followed, so Erin had to wait. And wait. For four whole days she'd had to wait.

The wait had been worth it.

Erin wasn't sure what Grandma had said to her mother — she had taken the phone call in her bedroom. But after a while Grandma had come to fetch her and Erin had gotten on the phone herself. Her mother had been very quiet, the way she was when she was upset, only Erin couldn't figure out what it was her mother had to be upset about. It was *her* hairy leg problem. Anyway, her mother had told Erin in her quiet voice that she'd had no idea the other kids were

151

teasing her and if the problem was so serious that it was ruining her life, of course she could shave her legs.

Erin had nodded into the phone, swallowed the whoop of joy in her throat, and told her mother several times that her life would simply be *ruined* if she didn't get rid of all the hateful hair on her legs.

It had been as easy as that.

The shaving part hadn't been so easy. Erin had nicked herself with a razor three times, twice on the leg with the blotches. But her grandmother had been there with Band-Aids and to answer all her questions about how to hold a razor and how much cream to use. Afterward they had celebrated with root beer floats on the back patio. It was the best present her grandmother had ever given her and Erin told her so.

Erin jumped out of bed and examined the blotchy leg. The blotches were still there but they were fading. With a few more Epsom salts baths, they should be completely gone by the weekend. By show day.

Blue stretched on his pillow and opened his mouth wide in an early morning yawn.

"Just a minute, Blue. I have to get dressed first." Automatically Erin reached for jeans, but her hand stopped mid-air when realization struck. Instead she pulled on pink biking shorts and a gray Nike T-shirt. She grinned at herself in the mirror. No more hiding her legs!

Her grandmother was wrong, Erin decided as she padded down the hall toward the back door to let Blue out. Shaving her legs *had* changed things. Just wait till Cassie saw her. And Rachel, too. Just wait until the dog show and September and maybe even working at the SPCA. She could wear skirts all year if she wanted to.

The reinvention was almost done. She touched the warts on her hand. They were almost gone, too. Soon she would be perfect.

There was a note on the kitchen counter propped against some apple Danishes. "Gone to see Sheila Jones," Erin read out loud. "Will be back by 10:30. Remember John comes at ten." Erin glanced at the clock. It was just after nine. She had an hour to eat and exercise Twister.

She put some food in Blue's dish and refreshed his water. She glanced out the window to see if the dog was ready to come in, but he was busy sniffing down by the apple tree. It was a nice morning. He would be outside for a while. She poured herself a large glass of orange juice, studied the Danishes to see which ones had the most icing, took two of them, and headed down the hall to the puppies.

"Okay, guys, okay!" Erin giggled as the puppies wobbled over to greet her. Her parents would be arriving for the dog show in just a few days and she couldn't wait for them to see the pups! She was sure they'd love them as much as she did. The little bundles of fur tumbled and fell over each other in their enthusiasm to get to Erin.

"In a few minutes." She sat down in the old green chair and took a bite out of a Danish. "Let me eat my breakfast first." She knew from experience that if she let the pups out now, they'd be all over her. And her breakfast. Grandma had just started introducing solid food. Apple Danishes weren't on their menu. Instead they got plain old baby Pablum mixed with a little yoghurt. Erin thought it was gross but the puppies loved it.

The pups were still terribly young but Erin imagined that she could already tell their personalities apart. There was Gumby, prancing and playing with one of the yellow puppies. Gumby, Erin decided, was a playful tease who liked to roughhouse. He was playing with a dog Erin called Honey. Honey was a sweet-natured female who loved to cuddle and lick.

She wiped the crumbs from her fingers, took a long gulp of orange juice, and went to work on her second Danish. She watched Gumby try to wrestle with Honey, but the dogs were still a little young for that. Soon another stocky yellow waddled over. Erin called him Arnold, after the famous actor. A fat black puppy began to bark. "You tell 'em, Fred," Erin said. That one reminded her of Fred Flintstone. He was the loudest of the bunch. Over in the corner was the puppy Grandma laughingly called the snob because she rarely joined in with the others. Erin thought she had the prettiest face of them all. She called her Mercedes, after the car.

And, of course there was Twister.

Where was Twister?

Quickly Erin scanned the crate. She couldn't see him. Maybe he was nursing? But Duchess was sitting on her haunches watching her puppies with a big Mama grin on her face. Erin could see her belly clearly. There was no nursing puppy.

The Danish stuck in Erin's throat. She stopped chewing. No! It couldn't be. She put the Danish down and forced herself to take a long, deep breath before her eyes slowly scanned the crate again. He had to be there somewhere!

14

There he was! In the corner, almost covered by the old gray blanket. Sleeping soundly. She could see the brace clearly now. It looked like two padded Popsicle sticks taped together. Her heart stopped pounding. She picked up her Danish and resumed chewing. For a minute she'd thought her grandmother had taken him away! But Twister was still there.

She licked her fingers and stood. "Get up, little guy," she said softly. "It's exercise time." The other puppies rushed at her. Twister still slept. "Okay!" She laughed as the puppies scrambled and fell over each other in their haste to get to the edge of the crate. "I'll play with you first."

After she finished with the other puppies, Blue was

barking for his breakfast. She let him in, and returned to the crate. Twister was still asleep. Leaning down, Erin gently removed the blanket and picked him up. He was a small ball of soft black fur. She cupped him under her chin and carried him to the old red blanket in the corner. "Let's see what you can do today," she murmured into his ear.

Twister yawned and stretched before giving her finger a gentle lick with his tiny, pink tongue. She smiled. But when she placed Twister on the ground, his legs wouldn't support his weight. He fell over. Her smile disappeared.

"Come on, sweetie," she coaxed. "Stand up." She slipped her fingers under Twister's belly and forced him up. The leg with the brace stood at attention but his three other legs folded under him. When she let go, Twister curled into a ball and laid his head on the blanket. "You're going to have to work extra hard today, Twister. The show's coming up and I'm going to be busy for a few days." She went to work on Twister's legs. She had the routine down pat by now. Massage, bend, stretch. Massage, bend, stretch. Every few minutes she would stop and encourage the puppy to stand.

Twister would fall back with a soft plop.

"Come *on*, Twister," she encouraged. "Just *try*." She frowned. Was it her imagination or was Twister worse today? Blue came in to see what she was doing, but Erin shooed him away. Massage, bend, stretch. Massage, bend, stretch.

"Erin?" John's voice traveled down the hall.

"Hi, John," she yelled back. She glanced at her watch. Yikes! An hour had passed. Once again she tried to get Twister to stand. Once again the puppy's legs wouldn't support his weight.

"Somehow I thought I might find you in here." John stood in the doorway, watching. "How's it going?"

"Good!" She made the word come out firm and strong. "Come on, Twister," she whispered. "Stand."

As soon as her fingers released him, the puppy's legs folded beneath him. His tiny head hit the blanket with a gentle plop.

"Doesn't look so good to me," John said.

"We just need to work on it some more," she said. "That's all."

John glanced at his watch. "Time's up for today, I'm afraid. Ready to go?"

She gave Twister a quick cuddle under her chin before lowering him into the crate. She made sure she left him as she found him, in the corner with the gray blanket tucked around him for comfort. "I guess."

"The exhibition grounds are open," John reminded her. "And they're probably setting up the field. Like I said last night, it's a great chance to get Blue used to the site before the show."

Erin took one last look at Twister before she left the room. She couldn't think about the show right now. Not with Twister needing her. "He just needs exercise, you know," she told John again. "He's going to be fine!"

"We'll talk in the car," he said.

He didn't believe her! Erin opened her mouth to argue but John was already out the door. Blue, knowing a car ride was just seconds away, was right behind him. She grabbed Blue's leash from the kitchen drawer, followed John to his Jeep, and slid into the passenger seat. Blue wedged himself between Erin and John and stared happily out the window. Blue loved going in the car almost as much as he loved running beside Erin's bike.

"It's true, you know," she said when they were on their way. "Twister *will* walk. I'll make him walk."

"It doesn't work that way, Erin." Blue's head was in the way and she couldn't see John's face, but he sounded sad. "There's a certain standard —"

"Of perfection," she interrupted hotly. "I know all about it."

The light up ahead turned green and John stepped on the gas. "There's that, yes, but what I was going to say was there's a certain standard of life," John explained mildly. "That puppy would never walk. He'd have to be carried all the time. What kind of life is that for a dog?"

When Erin was silent, John reached out and gave Blue's head a scratch. "Look at this guy. He's full of spunk and vinegar. He can't wait to get up in the morning and chase birds or bring you a stick. He'd be miserable if he couldn't do it. Just miserable."

"Twister will chase birds one day, too. I know he will!" Erin vowed swiftly. "And bring sticks."

"Maybe," John replied softly. "And maybe not."

Blue was panting from the heat in the Jeep and Erin rolled down her window. Adults didn't understand anything!

"The fact is, Erin, your grandma has a business to run," John continued. "And sometimes that means making hard decisions. Don't expect too much of her."

The only thing Erin expected was that Twister would walk. He *would* walk! She'd make sure of it.

John pulled into the parking lot at the Comox Valley Exhibition Grounds. "Looks like other people had the same idea." There were half a dozen cars and trucks scattered about. Erin watched an older woman carefully remove a pampered-looking cocker spaniel from the back of a blue sedan. Across the field she could see several men raising poles and tents. The door to the hall was open; animals and people were moving around inside.

The dog show was only three days away and she was going to be part of it! Erin's stomach did a tiny flip-flop. "Come on, Blue." She fastened the leash around the Lab's neck. "Be on your best behavior." She opened the door to the Jeep and jumped down.

"Remember Blue hasn't done this for a while," John reminded her as they walked in the direction of the hall. "He's bound to be excited. But this will give him a chance to sniff around before show day."

A Welsh corgi barked a greeting as they went inside. Blue barked back. Erin grinned. John frowned. Immediately she jerked on Blue's leash. "Quiet, Blue," she reprimanded him.

John nodded approvingly. "Good. Show him who's boss." He pointed to a table against the far wall. "We'll pick up the schedule before we check out the field."

The hall smelled like sneakers and sweat and old

gym clothes. Of gym class. Erin's heart began to pound. She hated gym class. But this wasn't gym class at all, she reminded herself. This was a dog show. A dog show where she wouldn't have to worry about hairy legs or tripping over her feet or making a fool of herself chasing some dumb ball around the room. All she had to do was show Mr. Lavender Blue.

"John! How are you?" A lady in a large flowery dress waddled out from behind the table. A big black Bouvier followed her. Erin could feel Blue straining to get close to the other dog so she leaned close to his ear. "Settle, Blue," she whispered.

"This must be Peggy's granddaughter." The woman had a voice bigger than her dress. "I'm Melissa McClanahan. But you can call me Missy. Everyone else does." Her wide face stretched into a fat grin and she held out her hand. The big black Bouvier opened his mouth in a giant yawn.

Erin fought back her giggle. "Hello." Politely she shook the woman's hand. "I'm Erin."

"Well, now, Erin, here's your schedule," Missy practically shouted as she handed Erin a large beige envelope. "As usual, juniors are on at noon. Nevertheless, I suggest you look everything over thoroughly just in case you have questions." Her voice echoed around the gym. "I'm the person to ask, you know." The Bouvier yawned again and this time Erin couldn't help herself. She giggled.

"Now I know you're nervous." Missy yelled. "But don't let that worry you. Everyone's nervous. My granddaughter will be showing in the same class as you. I'll make sure the two of you meet."

Maybe she couldn't hear very well, Erin thought. She couldn't see a hearing aid. Maybe she just liked to talk loudly. "Don't forget to bring a dog crate." Missy instructed. "He seems well behaved but, of course, you just never know what they'll do to you on show day, and it's always good to have somewhere to put them if they start to get excited." The Bouvier made a sound that was a cross between a huff and a sneeze.

"Oh, Alberto, bless you, darling."

Alberto laid down with a groan. Blue took a few steps forward and the two dogs sniffed noses.

Erin smirked at John. Alberto? Sounded like somebody on a hair commercial.

John hid his smile. "And how is Alberto these days?" he asked. "Last time I saw him, he had a bad hip."

The heavy-set woman gave the Bouvier an indulgent smile. "He recovered nicely, didn't you darling?" She gazed around the hall impatiently. "Veronica! Over here, Veronica." As Missy waved, the flowers on her dress danced up and down. "You'll get to meet my granddaughter after all," she beamed.

"Hello, Grandmother."

Erin recognized the voice. Her stomach sank to her toes. Maybe she was wrong. Slowly she turned. Her stomach fell out the end of her shoes. Just her luck!

It was the girl from the bakery. The girl with the purple streak in her hair and the neck like a giraffe.

The girl who'd said she had baboon legs.

"This is Veronica," Missy threw her arms around the girl and gave her a hug. "And Sugar, of course." She patted the golden Pomeranian under Veronica's arm. "You girls must be close to the same age. How wonderful that you'll have each other to spend time with."

Erin thought that she'd rather stick needles in her eyes.

Veronica nodded like she'd never seen Erin in her life. "Hello," she said pleasantly, playing with the pale pink bow attached to her dog's fur. "It's nice to meet you." Her eyes traveled down Erin's bare legs and back up again. Just then Blue wandered out from behind the table. "Nice . . ." Veronica hesitated, "dog." Her grin became smirky, mean.

"Thank you." It was Erin's turn to feign politeness.

"*Eii, eii, eii, eii, eii.*" Sugar the Pomeranian caught sight of Blue. She put back her ears and began to howl. Blue wagged his tail and walked toward her. "*Eii, eii, eii,*" the Pomeranian howled louder. Blue whined.

Veronica shushed her dog. Erin grinned. Sugar wasn't shushing.

"Now, now, Sugar," Missy fussed loudly. "It's all right, sweetheart." Blue whined a second time. Alberto merely yawned. A few of the other dogs in the hall, however, began to bark. Missy frowned. "Give her a biscuit, Veronica, darling. That always settles her down."

Veronica reached into the pocket of her black Nike track suit, pulled out a pale green dog biscuit, and shoved it under Sugar's nose. "*Eii, eii, eii, eii.*" Sugar twisted like a knot in Veronica's arms. She didn't want a biscuit. Veronica struggled to hold onto the dog. The dog bone dropped. So did the pale pink bow in Sugar's hair. Blue ambled over, sniffed the bow, and promptly ate the dog bone.

Erin and John laughed.

"*Eii, eii, eii, eii, eii.*" Sugar didn't like that at all. She clawed her way up to Veronica's shoulder and jumped. Her nails clicked against the floor as she ran for freedom.

Veronica turned the color of a radish and ran after her.

Missy's smile was apologetic. "Veronica is so good with her but these little dogs can be high-strung sometimes."

Erin snorted.

"Bless you." Missy thought Erin had sneezed.

"Yes, well, we must be off, too," John said, steering Erin and Blue toward the door.

"Good luck," Missy yelled after them. "Once Sugar gets used to Blue, I'm sure you and Veronica will become fast friends."

In your dreams, Erin thought. Instead she smiled and nodded.

Out on the field, dogs and owners were wandering around like they were out for a casual walk through the park. All except Sugar who was now making *eii, eii* noises at a German shepherd.

"Heel, Blue." Erin made sure Blue was in perfect form as he walked by the high-strung Sugar. She gave Veronica a wide, sunny smile. She was rewarded with a glare.

"It'll look different on Sunday," John said. "He's figuring out where the ring will go." He pointed to the middle of the field where an official-looking man with a clipboard and a tape measure was walking around murmuring to himself. "The judge will be there and the ring will be in front. You'll enter from somewhere back here and go through your paces. Blue will always be between you and the judge. There will be tables for the smaller dogs to pose on and the kennel area, too, of course."

A few birds scratched in the grass nearby, and Blue strained against the leash. He wanted to run. Erin released him. The birds scattered as the dog chased them. "I don't think we need to worry about the kennel area," Erin said. "Blue's pretty obedient." She called him and he came trotting back to her. "See?"

John leaned down and scratched Blue's ears. "He's a good dog, there's no question. But it can be pretty crazy around here on show day. The crate will give him somewhere to be quiet." He straightened. "Now let's find a place and put Blue through his paces."

They worked Blue for about twenty minutes before wandering the site and giving him a chance to familiarize himself with all the strange smells. Some of the other owners followed suit and soon there was a small group of dogs wandering happily over the grass. Even Sugar stopped making those horrible *eii, eii* noises, though she really wasn't very good at following commands, preferring to bark cheekily every time Veronica issued one. By the time they headed for home, Erin was feeling confident and excited.

"I think he's going to win," she told John as he drove past the Walker Flower Farm.

"Don't count your eggs before they're laid," John

said with a chuckle. "Blue's good but so are lots of other dogs."

"Blue's the best." Erin reached out to give the dog a hug. She was rewarded with a slurpy kiss across the side of her face.

"Better than Sugar at least." John gave her a mischievous grin.

Erin laughed. "That wouldn't be hard." Wait till Cassie heard about Veronica and Sugar.

The Jeep turned at the familiar Dove Creek Kennels sign and rolled past the holly bushes. "Looks like your grandma has company," John remarked.

Erin's eyes widened. It was a station wagon. Her parents' station wagon! A figure waved from the porch.

"Mom!" Erin yelled. She threw open the door and raced up the stairs. Excited by the sudden movement, Blue jumped down from the Jeep. "You're early," she shouted. And Blue barked in agreement.

* * * *

"So when your dad's new job was confirmed, we decided to take a few days off and come early," Erin's mom explained. "That way we'll be well rested and ready for the show." She reached out to touch Erin's hair for a second time. "I just *love* that color on you."

Erin grinned. "Thanks, Mom." Her mother hadn't said a word about her legs and she hadn't noticed that her warts were gone, but she had noticed the hair as soon as Erin had jumped from the Jeep. Mom's mouth had fallen open. She had stretched out her hand and touched it like she had never seen Erin's hair before, and her father had made a crack about Erin being too young to mess with stuff like that. But then Grandma had come outside, heard everything and came to her rescue by saying how nice it was that Erin had picked such a pretty color instead of the blues and greens some young people were choosing. Dad had shut his mouth and Mom had smiled and agreed. And that had been that.

Erin scooped up the last piece of her blueberry cheesecake, the awesome dessert, that her mother had brought special delivery from the North Shore bakery. "Youftshppes."

"Finish your mouthful, bug-face." Erin could tell her father wasn't really angry; in fact, he looked happier and more relaxed than Erin had seen him in a long time.

"You have to see the puppies!" She licked the blueberry glaze from her fork as she glanced from her father to her mother. "You haven't seen them yet, have you?"

"We asked but Grandma said we had to wait for you."

"Something about you assisting in the delivery room." Her father's eyes twinkled above his coffee cup.

"You should have seen it," Erin said as she led her parents down the hall. "It was great!"

Duchess greeted them with a thump of her tail, and the movement woke Arnie and Gumby. Erin reached for Gumby and cradled him against her chest. "See?" she said, holding out his foot. "I put the nail polish on his toe."

Arnie began to whimper and Mom laughed. "Come here," she said, lifting the stocky yellow lab from the crate.

Erin pointed to the corner where several of the puppies were curled up together. "That's Mercedes, she's the prettiest. And Honey, she's the nicest. And Fred is the loudest."

"That must be Twister." Dad gestured to the lone black puppy eyeing them from the other side of the crate.

She nodded. She put Gumby down and reached for him. "He has a problem with his leg."

"Grandma told us."

Erin held Twister against her cheek. The puppy didn't squirm like the rest of the litter; he barely moved in her hand. His fur was soft, like the rabbit's foot charm she kept in her desk at school. "I want to take him home!"

Erin's parents were both silent.

"I've been working with him every single day. I can make him walk, I know I can. I'll work with him twice a day even," she promised. "You said when I showed some responsibility I could have a pet. I've been helping Grandma a lot and working with John and Blue every day and I'm going to try and get on as a volunteer at the SPCA this fall. A *volunteer*," she stressed again. "Which is pretty responsible since everybody knows kids need money but I don't care about that because all I want to do is work with dogs!" She was out of breath.

Her parents glanced at each other and then back at Erin. Her mother's mouth was set in what Erin called her "crumble smile" — the smile she used when she was trying not to cry. Her father fiddled with his earlobe. Dad only fiddled with his earlobe when he was uncomfortable.

Erin stroked Twister and whispered in his ear. This morning when she'd done that he had twitched and licked at her fingers. This afternoon he did nothing. He was soft and limp in her hand. "Twister will be fine," she told her parents. "He just needs extra love and attention, that's all!" She stroked his tiny head.

"He's badly injured," Mom said softly. "We can't take care of him."

"*I* can. You don't have to do anything!"

"Let me have a look," her father said gruffly. He held out his hand.

She handed Twister to her father. "Careful," she cautioned as her father held Twister high in the air and studied him.

"He has a nice face."

"Steve," Mom warned.

Erin's heart jumped. Dad liked him. She could tell! "He's a beauty, Dad. A real beauty. He'd make a great pet. Just look how quiet he is. How laid-back. He wouldn't be a jumper. Not this one."

Her father stroked Twister's head for a minute before putting him back into the corner of the crate. "It's up to Grandma, bug-face. She may not be letting him go home with anyone." He straightened and reached for Erin. "Besides, first things first." He gave her shoulders a squeeze. "I understand there's a dog show to win!"

15

"Senior Novice." A nasally sounding voice called. "Would all those participating in Senior Novice please bring themselves and their dogs to the starting position? Thank you very much."

"That's you!" Cassie gave her a hard hug.

Erin nodded and licked her lips. Her mouth was dry and toasty, filled with a stale, leftover popcorn taste. The taste of nervousness.

The wind caught a corner of her hair. Nervously she smoothed it back into place. A light breeze swept through the crowd at the Comox Valley Exhibition Grounds, cooling the hot midday sun, gently lifting the bottoms of skirts and tugging playfully at sun hats.

John led Erin and Cassie past clusters of dogs and

owners to the show ring and the nearby seats. Blue strolled happily beside them.

"You look great," Cassie whispered in her ear. "The perfect reinvention worked!"

Erin grinned. It had been worth it. Every single glob of that smelly henna, every painful tweeze of her eyebrows, all that horrible cream that had burned her legs. Even her warts were gone, shrunk to tiny pinprick-sized dots on her hand.

Yes, Erin Morris had been reinvented in time for the Comox Valley Dog Show. "Thanks, Cass," she whispered back.

"It's time." John came to a stop outside the ring.

Erin's heart was pounding so hard she was sure if she looked down she would see her multicolored top moving in time to the beat. She smoothed the short white denim skirt and reached for Blue's leash.

"You can do this," John reminded her again as he fastened the number card around the top of her arm. "You're well-prepared and so is Blue."

A monarch butterfly circled in the sunlight a few feet away and Blue lunged for it. Erin pulled on his leash. "Behave, Blue!" she ordered.

"Good luck." John gave her arm one last pat and then he was gone. Cassie gave her the thumbs-up sign and followed him to their seats.

With a firm hold on Blue, she headed for the ring. *Thrump, thrump, thrump.* She wondered if anyone had ever died from a pounding heart before. Her mother and father waved from their seats as she went by. Grandma gave her a grin and blew her a kiss. Erin gave them all a weak smile.

All of a sudden this dog show seemed like a really dumb idea!

Even with the perfect reinvention.

She felt like she was walking through a field of mashed potatoes as she walked toward her starting position. What if she tripped over her feet like she sometimes did?

Or worse, tripped over Blue?

Squished him flat like a pancake!

Her skirt would fly up in the air.

So what if she didn't have warts on her hands anymore? Or hair on her legs. So what if her hair was bouncy and plum perfect?

Everyone would know Erin Morris was the same old klutz she had always been.

So much for perfection.

"Number please?" It was the same man who had surveyed the field just a few days earlier.

"Forty-four," she mumbled.

The man frowned. "Pardon?"

"Forty-four!"

"Hmm." The man scanned down his clipboard. "Right, there you are. Erin Morris." He made a check beside her name. "You're beside McClanahan." He gestured toward the middle of the line. "The girl wearing turquoise, with the golden brown Pomeranian."

Great! Just her luck there were no mid-sized dogs between the Pomeranian and Blue. She was going to be stuck beside Sugar for the entire show.

"Eiii, eii, eii."

Erin swallowed a nervous giggle. Then again, the other dog was bound to make Blue look good! "Hello," she said, taking her spot by Veronica. "Isn't it nice that our dogs will be beside each other?" She gave the girl an innocent smile.

Sugar began to do contortions again. *"Eii, eii, eii,"* she yelped, her buggy eyes firmly fastened on Blue.

"Not really," Veronica said rudely. She stuck her warthog nose in the air. "My dog doesn't like your dog."

So much for friendliness. "We can't all have good taste," Erin snapped.

"Eii, eii, eii." Sugar was getting louder. People were staring. Erin watched as Veronica clamped a large, square hand over the Pomeranian's mouth. "Shut up, Sugar," Veronica hissed.

The line filled up quickly. Behind Erin was a tall, thin boy with a beautiful Boxer named Oscar. The boy gave Erin a shy smile. Oscar and Blue wagged their tails at each other but seemed perfectly content to stand quietly and wait for the judging to begin.

Not Sugar. Sugar yelped every time a new dog ventured within twenty yards of her territory. Veronica McClanahan was getting more and more frustrated. I ought to feel sorry for her, Erin thought. But she couldn't feel sorry for someone who'd said she had baboon legs. She wouldn't!

The judge walked into the ring. Erin straightened her shoulders and tightened her hold on Blue's leash.

"Ladies and gentlemen, we are about to begin."

"Steady, Blue," Erin urged. Her heart started pounding again. She exchanged glances with Oscar's owner who whispered "good luck." Erin smiled and nodded her thanks. Sugar started howling.

"Take your animals into the ring, please," the judge instructed. "And take up your positions."

Erin and Blue were right in the middle of the pack. She waited almost a minute for the line to begin moving and, once it did, she let Veronica and Sugar get a good start. The last thing she wanted was Blue spooked because of that dog's yipping.

Sugar wasn't howling at Blue. She was howling at the Great Dane in front of her. And making such a fuss, in fact, that Veronica was forced to pull her along.

It was like walking behind a pull toy.

As she passed the judge, Erin pretended she was perfectly used to walking behind pull toys. She flashed the man a confident smile.

"Tail up," she urged Blue. Blue's tail went higher.

"Steady on," she coached. Blue's pacing was smooth; his gait excellent.

"Good work, Blue." Erin heaped praise all over the dog once they were still and he was in the correct position. She reached into her skirt pocket for a dog biscuit and he crunched it enthusiastically.

"*Eii, eii, eii.*" Sugar didn't like the sound of Blue's crunching. "*Eii, eii, eii.*"

"Would you please refrain from feeding your animal?" Veronica McClanahan sniffed. "Sugar doesn't like it."

"*Eii, eii, eii.*" By the sound of it, Sugar didn't like much.

"Would number 11 please control her animal?" the judge asked loudly. All eyes turned to Erin's end of the field.

Number 11. Veronica McClanahan. Erin watched the girl's hand clamp itself around Sugar's face. This time Erin did feel sorry. For the dog. Sugar just wasn't show material.

"Bait and stack your dogs, please," the judge said next.

Stacking was simply a matter of putting your dog in the proper standing position. Erin had practiced it on Blue hundreds of times. Now she corrected Blue's front foot, lifted his chin, and stretched his tail into place. She made herself go slow and steady. She could feel the judge watching her. So far, so good.

Veronica, on the other hand, was struggling with Sugar, who had to be stacked on a table. The little dog was skidding and sliding, running from one hand to another like they were playing a game. How embarrassing! Erin fought back a smile and looked away.

"Perhaps we'll have the animals walk a pattern in a group first so they have a chance to work off some steam." The judge's eyes swept over the dogs, lingering a little too long on poor old Sugar. "The triangle pattern, please."

Blue's favorite pattern and hers, too, Erin thought. So far, so good. The line began to move. Oscar and his owner started to walk. Erin counted off five seconds before she issued the command to Blue. The black Lab moved out in a straight line. His head was up and his tail was proudly displayed. He took the first turn perfectly. And the second. Erin slowed as she passed the judge, just as John had instructed.

"Perfect! Good boy." Erin scratched him vigorously behind the ears. She glanced over to the spectators and caught a glimpse of Cassie, wildly waving her arms in encouragement, her grandmother grinning broadly, and John giving her the thumbs-up signal. Erin grinned. She and Blue had to be getting a good score. They just had to be.

"Assume your positions, please. Individual judging is about to begin."

The line stretched out, with dogs and owners spaced neatly apart. The judge headed for the middle of the line — straight for Veronica McClanahan and Sugar. Erin looked at Blue and held her finger to her lips. "Quiet, Blue," she murmured as she continued to bait and stack him.

"And your dog's name is?" The judge gave Veronica a friendly smile.

Sugar jumped off the table. "*Eii, eii, eii, eii.*" The Pomeranian lunged for the man's feet.

Erin tried hard not to giggle. Blue shuffled his feet; Erin quickly moved him back into position.

"Sugar." Veronica lifted Sugar up and held her tight. "Er, Sugar McClanahan the Third. And normally she's very well behaved. I'm not sure what has gotten into her this afternoon."

Erin looked at Oscar's owner and rolled her eyes. He grinned back.

"I see. Yes." The judge offered Veronica a sympathetic smile. "And what is her breed?"

"Pomeranian," Veronica said, but before she could continue, Sugar took over. "*Eii, eii, eii, eii, eii.*" The girl slapped her hand over Sugar's nose and raised her voice. "She's spooked by some of these other bigger dogs." She gave Blue a dirty look before she turned back to the judge. "She took all firsts in her puppy class last summer."

Erin smirked. Puppy class for noise and rudeness, probably.

"That's fine, Miss." The judge was getting impatient. "Stack her again, please."

Veronica set Sugar into position on the table. "Stay," she ordered in a wavery voice. But the dog yapped twice and then jumped up and bit Veronica's nose before squatting and peeing on the table.

The judge winced and looked away. "I'll come back to you," he promised, moving toward Erin and Blue.

He stopped between them. His eyes were on Blue. Blue eyed him back. His tail gave a friendly wag but he was quiet. The judge smiled and turned to Erin. "Dog's name, please?" he asked.

"Mr. Lavender Blue," she answered swiftly. "From Dove Creek Kennels in Courtenay." She was kneeling beside Blue, her hand holding the leash steady at his neck, her other hand behind his tail. Blue looked great! She knew he did. His front and hindquarters were perfectly placed, just like John had taught her. His head was forward; he was holding his position patiently.

The judge nodded approvingly, circled Blue, and made a few comments in his book. "Very nice." He patted Blue on the head and smiled. "I have a few questions for your handler now. You can relax for a few minutes."

Blue wagged his tail again. Erin saw John grinning and forced herself to breathe.

"What group does Blue belong to?" the judge asked.

"The sporting group," Erin answered promptly. "Which consists of pointers and setters, retrievers and spaniels."

"And what are the main characteristics of your dog?"

Erin recited from memory. The judge nodded approvingly.

"What is the difference between a golden Lab and a yellow Lab?"

Erin grinned. It was a trick question and she was prepared for it. "There's no such thing as a golden Lab," she replied swiftly. "There are yellow Labradors and golden Retrievers, but golden Retrievers are a separate breed."

The judge flashed a smile. After a few more questions about breed history, temperament, and health problems, he said, "Let's examine Blue, shall we?"

Erin bent down and the judge continued to question her. "Show me his hip, please."

Erin pointed.

"His tail?"

Too easy. Erin pointed again.

"How about his stifle?"

Erin hesitated. The stifle was on the leg somewhere. She ran her hand up from Blue's foot and when she reached his hock, she remembered. "There," she said, pointing to Blue's knee.

"Good." The judge nodded. "And where is his breastbone?"

His breastbone. Erin frowned. Dogs didn't have breastbones. Or did they? She stared at Blue's chest. What if she was wrong? "I don't . . ." she stopped. So she would be wrong. She had to take that chance. "Dogs don't have breastbones," she said.

"Well done!" the judge said with a satisfied look on his face. He turned his attention back to Blue. "Would you show me his bite, please?"

Erin froze. The mouth exam hadn't been a sure thing. John had said sometimes judges did it and sometimes they didn't. Blue hated having his mouth touched. And no one could get him to open it if he didn't want to — no one, not even John. And especially Erin. Brushing his teeth every day had been torture.

She could feel the eyes on her: dogs' eyes, peoples' eyes, the judge's eyes. They were waiting for her to issue the command. She couldn't. She just *couldn't*.

If she did, Erin knew exactly what would happen. There would be a big fuss, and the winning ribbon, the ribbon she and Blue had worked so far for, wouldn't go to him at all. It would go to some other dog.

"Well," the judge said brightly. "Come on."

"I . . ." Erin opened her mouth to explain but then stopped herself. John had told her over and over again that no matter what Blue did, she should never make excuses for him. Like Veronica had done for Sugar.

"Okay." Taking a deep breath, Erin put one hand

on top of Blue's head and the other under his chin. The judge knelt down to take a close look.

Blue would not open his mouth.

Come on, Blue, Erin urged silently. *We've come this far. Don't blow it now!* She worked his mouth with her hands.

Blue's mouth still wouldn't budge.

Oscar's owner gave her a sympathetic look. Erin stared hard at Blue, willing him to open his mouth. The dog stared stubbornly back.

The judge glanced up at Erin. "Do you say something special to him?"

"Not really." Erin squeezed the dog's chin. "Open, Blue," she said sternly.

Blue clenched his teeth.

Desperation powered Erin's hands. She wedged her fingers into Blue's mouth. "Open!" She pried his jaw apart.

Blue opened his mouth.

The judge nodded vigorously. "Very good." He leaned over and gave his teeth a leisurely examination.

Hurry up, hurry up! Erin chanted under her breath. *Before he snaps his jaw shut again.*

Finally the judge straightened. "Thank you," he said. "Walk Mr. Lavender Blue in an L pattern, please."

Off they went. It wasn't Blue's best walk. He was getting tired. Erin was still shaking from the mouth examination. Blue went too fast in a few spots and Erin stumbled over a rock in front of the spectators.

She could squish him flat like a pancake.

Her skirt could fly into the air.

And everyone would know she was the same old klutz.

"Thank you." The judge nodded when she returned. She'd blown it. For sure! Erin watched the judge move on to Oscar and his owner. She paid little attention as the other dogs and their owners went through the routine of baiting, stacking, and answering questions. She was reviewing Blue's performance. Her own performance. Maybe she hadn't blown it. Maybe she still had a chance.

She worried over every single little detail.

She wondered where she would place.

"Please stand by," the announcer said. "The winners will be revealed momentarily."

She could feel a thin line of sweat trickling down her shoulder blades to the small of her back. Her forehead was damp, her hands clammy. Blue was getting restless. She baited and stacked him again. He looked up at her with big, trusting eyes. Now what? he seemed to be saying. "Shhh," she whispered. Soon it would be over. Soon she would know.

"Before making my final decision, I'd like to ask the handlers to take their dogs around the ring once more," the judge announced.

Erin's heart thumped wildly. Judges only did that when they were having trouble making a decision. Handlers and dogs began to move. A sudden hush fell over the crowd. Everyone seemed to know how close the decision was. Even Sugar was strangely quiet and well behaved. The walk around the ring seemed to take forever. Erin felt like she was walking through mashed potatoes all over again. Finally it was over. Dogs and owners returned to their standing positions.

The judge looked at each couple in turn. Handler and dog. Handler and dog. Erin licked her lips nervously. That last walk had been perfect, but the one before hadn't. She'd almost tripped then. Maybe she and Blue would come in second. It was probably about as close to perfect as she was going to get.

"I am pleased to —" A wild bout of coughing overcame the man and he stopped.

Not now! Blue stirred restlessly and Erin jerked on his leash. "Sit still," she whispered.

"Excuse me." He accepted a glass of water and took a long drink. "That's better." The judge gave one last cough and smiled at the crowd. "As I was about to say, I am pleased to announce my decision."

The judge walked across the ring toward her. Erin felt lightheaded, dizzy. He stood in front of her and pointed. "First," he pronounced loudly. He moved down the line, pointing out second and third in quick succession.

At first Erin wasn't sure she'd heard right.

Everyone clapped, which made Sugar start her *eii, eii* noises again, and then Blue barked, which made everyone laugh. It was all very confusing until Erin saw Veronica glaring at her and the thin boy with the shy smile motioning her forward.

She and Blue had won!

Erin was floating. She wasn't walking through mashed potatoes anymore. She was floating through clouds. Grinning harder than she'd ever grinned in her life. Grinning so hard she was sure her face was going to crack.

"Congratulations." The judge moved the winning dogs and their handlers into place and then quickly handed out ribbons — a large, blue first place ribbon for her and Blue. Just as she was being ushered away for a picture, Erin looked up and saw Cassie waving wildly. . . . her parents clapping and grinning . . . John looking happy and proud. . . and her grandmother jumping up and down with excitement.

She had won. She and Blue had *really* won.

And then Erin tasted it! The taste of perfection. It filled her mouth and bubbled down her throat. It was better than anything she had ever tasted before. Better than the best cheesecake from the North Shore bakery. Better than her favorite ice cream float. Better than blueberries fresh from the bush. Or corn on the cob bursting with summer sweetness.

Perfection was something Erin Morris had never tasted before. And it was a taste she would never forget.

Blue was perfect. She was perfect. There was another dog show in Campbell River next week. That was perfect, too. Because Blue would win again. She knew it.

She had tasted perfection. And she wanted to taste it again.

16

"I knew you could do it," Grandma declared, beaming from the easy chair in the corner of the living room. "There wasn't a doubt in my mind that you and Blue would win." She reached down and gave Blue's head a scratch. "He's such a champ, this one." Blue was tired of being the center of attention. He yawned and stretched out for a well-earned nap.

John scraped up the last of the crumbs from the chocolate cake he'd bought to celebrate. "I was worried when I realized the judge was doing that mouth exam." He licked his fork and put his plate on the coffee table.

Erin started to giggle. "Me, too," she said. "Especially when Blue wouldn't open his mouth right away." She had just finished talking on the phone with Rachel and was sprawled out on the floor beside Blue. "And then he walked too fast during the L pattern and I tripped on that rock." She shook her head in wonder. "At first I was so sure we'd win but not after that."

"You did a fabulous job, darlin'. You helped me out and showed a great deal of responsibility at the same time." Grandma put her coffee down on the nearby table. "Blue's come a long way in the weeks you've worked with him. This win has been great for him. If he keeps on like this, he'll be earning more ribbons than I have space for." She giggled at her own joke.

"Your dad and I are very proud of you," Mom said. "And not just because you and Blue won, either."

"That's right, bug-face." Her father had taken up his familiar after-dinner pose, reclining in the corner of the couch, one arm stretched out beside him. "You worked hard this summer and it shows."

She brought her knees under her chest, folded her arms around them, and rocked back and forth. "So can I have a dog then? Pleeeease?" She glanced from her father to her mother. "Let me have Twister! I can take care of him. I can make him walk. I know I can. Pleeeease?"

"I'm not sure you'll have time for a dog," Dad said, "you're going to be pretty busy come September."

Erin rolled her eyes. "I can handle grade seven, Dad, you just wait and see." She had just spent the last half hour on the phone filling Rachel in on all the changes — her plum perfect hair, her smoother-than-smooth legs, and her wart-free left hand. Not to mention the dog show win!

"Er, that's not quite what I meant." Dad cleared his throat. "I didn't want to tell you before the show in case you got distracted, but I heard back from the SPCA. They've got a volunteer spot for you this September, if you still want it."

"Want it?" Erin shrieked, rocking back and forth even faster than before. "Of course, I want it!" First the win, now this. Everything was working out perfectly! "I'll be able to volunteer at the SPCA and handle grade seven *and* look after Twister. Pleeeeeaaaaase?" she begged again.

Her mother and father looked at each other before looking at Grandma.

Erin's heart skittered into her throat. They *were* thinking about it. "I'll take such good care of him. I'll teach him to walk. I'll groom him and work with him. I'll even train him, just like John taught me. Maybe next year we can do three or four shows together!" She stopped rocking and leaned close to her grandmother. "Please, Grandma? I promise you I'll take perfect care of Twister. Extra perfect care."

Grandma looked at Erin for a long time without saying anything. "I'm afraid that's not possible, darlin'," she finally said.

"What do you mean, not possible?"

There was a look in her grandmother's eyes that Erin had never seen before. "Dr. Maartens came and took Twister away," she said softly. "While we were at the show."

At first Erin misunderstood. "But he'll be back,

right? After the doctor examines him again."

Grandma shook her head. "Erin, Twister was failing badly. He hadn't been eating. His heart was giving out." Grandma's eyes were overly bright, like she was about to cry. "He'd never walk. It just wasn't possible. We put him down, darlin'. It was the best thing for him."

"No!" Horrified, she stared at her grandmother. "How could you? He was a beautiful, innocent puppy. So gentle and quiet." There was a huge lump in Erin's throat but she forced the words to move around it. "He would have made a perfect pet. Just perfect."

"You don't understand, darlin'. . ." Grandma tried to explain.

"You're right," Erin's voice began to climb. "I don't understand. That was a mean, awful thing to do."

"Erin." Her father's voice issued a warning.

"There will be other dogs, Erin," Mom said.

"Your grandmother did what she had to do," John added.

The lump in Erin's throat grew bigger. The tears gathered behind her eyes. "I don't care!" she yelled rudely.

Blue jumped up and whined.

Erin stared at them all: her grandmother and John, her mother and father. They were so big. So mean! And Twister was so little! So helpless. "I'm going to Cassie's!" She jumped up and bolted for the back door. Cassie would understand. She always did.

"Wait until you're calm," Grandma urged.

"Wait at least five —"

The rest of her mother's words were lost in the slamming of the door. "Come on, Blue!" Erin grabbed her bike from the shed. "We're going for a ride."

She was out the gate and down the road before she realized she had forgotten her helmet. And Blue's harness. The springer bounced gently, its unattached end slapping softly against the road.

"Too bad," she muttered under her breath as she pumped the pedals on the bike. She wasn't going back. Not now. Not later, either. She wasn't going to calm down anytime soon. She was going to see if she could stay overnight at Cassie's place.

Blue was as happy as Erin was sad. He raced ahead of her, jumping at a monarch butterfly, barking at a sparrow. He loved running beside the bike. And tonight he loved his freedom.

The wind whipped her hair into a stinging frenzy. Impatiently, she pushed it away. Faster, faster, faster, she pedaled. Poor Twister. Poor, poor Twister.

There was a movement in the bushes across the road. She slowed for the corner and glanced left. There was a flash of beige, a tip of white.

A deer!

Blue saw it, too.

"Wait, Blue," she warned. She could hear a car up ahead.

"Woof!" The dog charged.

Brakes screeched.

"Blue!"

There was a thud of flesh hitting metal.

For a minute there was stillness. And then the air filled with the piercing sound of an animal howling in desperate and confused agony.

17

"Noooooooooooooo!" Erin's bike went one way; she went the other. She stared down at the still, dark ball curled up against the base of a tire. He should be barking . . . chasing butterflies . . . running in circles around her bike. "Blue! Get up, Blue! Get up!" If only she'd put him on the springer.

Helpless, Blue looked up at her. His dark eyes were huge and shiny. His howls had turned to soft whimpers. From very far away came the sound of a car door slamming . . . the sound of footsteps approaching.

All Erin could see or hear or think about was Blue. She threw herself on the ground beside him. "Blue. Oh, Blue." She buried her face in his fur of his neck. "Blue. Mr. Lavender Blue. My champion. My love. I'm sorry.

I'm so sorry," she sobbed. "I should have remembered the harness and put you on the springer. It's all my fault. I'm sorry, Blue. I'm so sorry."

Blue whimpered again. She could see something starting to stain the ground underneath him. Blood! All of a sudden her stomach felt queasy; she could taste the chocolate cake she'd had for dessert.

"We have to call for help," a shaky voice said.

Erin brushed the tears from her eyes and looked up. Sheila Jones, her face round and frightened, stared down at her. Actually she was staring at Blue. "I . . . I . . . I didn't see him. I wasn't going fast. I'm sure I wasn't. I was thinking about the lovely dog I'm pick-ing up next week from your grandmother. The one you call Arnie." Sheila Jones was babbling. In her hand was a cellular phone.

A phone! Erin reached out to grab it but Sheila Jones was gesturing so wildly Erin couldn't get it. And the woman was still talking. "We have to call for help," she said again, her shocked eyes remaining on Blue. "He just ran right out in front of me. I felt the bump the same time I saw him. He was running very fast. Where is his leash?" Sheila Jones seemed to remember Erin was there. She looked up. Her face was the same gray as the gravel on the road. "Did it come off?" She glanced around. "Where is it?"

Erin gulped. "I . . ."

Blue whimpered. Erin turned back to Blue. She laid a hand on the dog's neck. She didn't want to be away from him for a minute. "Phone 911," she cried over her shoulder. "The police. Or . . . or somebody."

Sheila Jones seemed incapable of speaking. "I . . . I . . ."

Blue let out a howl.

Erin's stomach lurched. The dog needed help now. She'd have to do it herself!

She snatched the phone from her grandmother's friend. Her fingers were shaking. It took her three tries just to punch out 911. Her voice quavered as she spoke. "Just before the Walker Flower Farm," she told the operator. "On Dove Creek Road. Hurry!" she urged.

"There, Blue." She leaned over and rubbed her face against Blue's ear. Her tears made his black fur gleam in the dusky evening light. "The operator said she'd call the SPCA. They'll send a truck soon. I promise!" The blood stain was growing. Erin wouldn't look. Of course, there was blood, she told herself as she took a deep breath. There was a cut for sure. Maybe even a broken leg. But help was coming. Blue would be fine.

Everything would be fine!

"They're coming," she reassured Sheila Jones, who was leaning against the car, holding her hand over her mouth and looking like she was going to be sick. For a minute Erin almost felt sorry for her.

The woman's head bobbed up and down vigorously. "Good," she said. "I'm so sorry . . ." She stopped and pressed her trembling lips together. Her eyes remained fixed on Erin. She knew she was trying not to look at Blue. "Your grandmother is my —" Sheila Jones stopped again. "I'm so sorry," she repeated.

Her grandmother! She had to call her grandmother. Erin's fingers were steady now as she punched out the familiar number. Dogs got hit by cars all the time. Blue would be fine. Just fine! At the sound of her grandmother's "Hello," Erin's courage flew. She began to sob. What if . . . what if Blue wasn't fine? It would be all her fault.

"Grrr . . . rrranndma."

"What is it? What's wrong?" Grandma's voice was sharp with alarm.

"I'm I'm I'm sorry."

"What is it?" Grandma repeated. "What's happened?"

Erin swallowed her tears. "There's been an accident."

"Are you all right? Where are you? Are you hurt? Just calm down, darlin'. Speak slowly."

"I'm . . . I'm on the road to Cassie's. There was a deer. A car. Sheila Jones. It's Blue." The tears started again. "He's hurt, Grandma. There's blood." Erin glanced down. "A . . . a lot of blood. I'm so scared."

"We'll be right there, darlin'. Right there!"

And they were. It seemed like Erin had just handed the phone back when John's Jeep came rushing up the road. Her mother flew to her side, while John, Grandma and her father ran to Blue. Sheila Jones hovered between the two groups, wringing her hands and saying over and over again, "He just ran right out in front of me. I felt the bump the same time I saw him."

"Are you okay, sweetheart?" Mom cupped Erin's face with her hands before pulling back to give her arms and legs a quick once over. "Did you get hit, too? Are you all right?"

She nodded. "I'm fine. But Blue . . ." She wiped her eyes with the back of her hand. "Blue's hurt." John and Peggy were huddled around the dog; Erin couldn't see what they were doing.

"I know," her mother said softly. "We called for help but it sounds like you beat us to it. Good girl," she added.

She wasn't a good girl at all! She was awful. She'd forgotten to put Blue on the springer. She didn't deserve to have a dog of her own. Anger rushed through Erin and filled her mouth with hot bitterness. She was angry at herself for her forgetfulness. And she was also angry at Sheila Jones for coming along the road when she did. She glared at the woman who was now talking to Dad in a quick, scared voice. "Came running out of nowhere," Erin heard her say. "She was going too fast," she whispered to her mother. "Way too fast!"

"Don't worry about that right now, Erin," her mother said soothingly. "Let's deal with Blue first."

"I should have put him on the springer, Mom," Erin whispered. "It's my fault, too. What if . . . what if—" Her voice cracked. "What if Blue dies?"

Mom's arms went around Erin. "Look," she urged. "See that?"

Erin looked. Coming around the corner was an SPCA truck with the words "Animal Hospital" printed on the bottom.

"Help's here. They're going to do everything they can to make sure Blue makes it. Everything!" her mother promised fiercely.

* * * *

Erin sat hunched in the corner of the couch, staring at the hands on her grandmother's old mantel clock: 10:30. Her grandmother had promised to phone as soon as Dr. Maartens looked at Blue. That had been almost two hours ago.

"You should get to bed, bug-face," Dad said, looking up from his crossword puzzle.

"You said I could wait till Grandma called." Erin pulled her knees under her chin and rocked slowly back and forth. How could a day that had started out so perfectly turn out so perfectly awful? First Twister.

Now Blue.

Twister had been horrible. Awful.

But what had happened to Blue was worse. Erin remembered the words John had used to describe Blue in the car just a few days ago. *Full of spunk and vinegar.* Then she thought of Blue lying in a heap on the side of the road. Whimpering. Staring up at her with those big, shiny eyes. His spunk and vinegar were gone.

And it was all her fault. Sheila Jones insisted she hadn't been speeding. She had been driving below the speed limit. She always did.

Erin believed her.

Blue's accident was all her fault. There was no one else to blame.

If only she had remembered the harness. If only Blue hadn't seen the deer. If only . . . if only.

"Here's your hot chocolate." Mom laid a tray on the coffee table and glanced at the clock herself. "I think eleven o'clock is late enough," she told Erin gently, handing her a mug. "How about it?"

"No." Erin shook her head. "You said I could wait till they called. And they promised they'd call as soon as they had news."

Please, God, let Blue be okay, she begged silently. *I'll never ask for anything else as long as I live. Please, God, don't let Blue die. Let him be full of spunk and vinegar again.*

"Drink up," her mother urged.

Erin tapped a marshmallow and watched it slowly dissolve into the brown liquid. Everything had been so perfect . . . the perfect reinvention . . . the perfect dog show . . . the perfect Mr. Lavender Blue. But not now. Not anymore.

A stream of light shot through the open window. Headlights. They were back! Erin jumped up so fast, her hot chocolate slopped over the side of the cup.

"Careful!" Mom warned as she took the cup from her.

Dad put down his crossword puzzle book and stood. One Jeep door slammed and then the other.

Erin waited. For a second she almost expected Blue to come running ahead as he always did. But he didn't. Not tonight.

"Come on, bug-face." Her father dropped his arm casually on Erin's shoulder and propelled her in the direction of the door. "Let's go see how he is."

Grandma and John were leaning against the side of the Jeep, talking quietly. The light from the living room dusted their faces in a pale glow, but it wasn't bright enough to tell Erin how they were feeling.

They were quiet as Erin and her mother and father approached.

How is he? Erin wanted to scream. But she was silent, embarrassed that she had caused this trouble . . . this pain.

"How is he?" Erin's father spoke for her.

"He lost a lot of blood." John sounded tired.

Erin swallowed. *Please, God*, she begged again. *Please, God.* "Is he . . . is he?"

"He's alive," Grandma whispered softly in the darkness. "But he's in pretty bad shape. Let's go inside." She moved toward the stairs. "I need to sit down."

"I just made hot chocolate," Mom said after Grandma sank slowly into a kitchen chair. "How about some?"

John shook his head as he took the chair beside Grandma. "No thanks."

"Sounds good," Grandma said wearily. "I'm feeling a touch cold tonight."

Erin had never seen her grandmother look so pale or so worn out. The morning after the puppies were born she had looked tired. Tonight her brown eyes were shadowed and her face was haggard; she looked exhausted.

Don't cry. Don't cry! Erin fought back the tears that were gathering again. "I'm so sorry," she whispered to her grandmother as she stood hesitantly in the doorway. "It's all my fault and I'm so, so sorry."

Grandma nodded. She opened her mouth to speak and then shut it. Her eyes stayed on the mug of chocolate Erin's mother placed in front of her.

Say something, Erin wanted to scream. *Anything!*

John spoke instead. "Accidents happen," he said gently. "We all know that." He took Grandma's hand.

"How is . . . will Blue . . . will he be all right?" Erin asked.

Her grandmother finally raised her eyes to look at Erin. "The operation's over. We'll just have to wait and see how Blue does through the night." Grandma's voice was strained.

Erin's heart began to pound. "Operation?"

Grandma nodded. "They amputated, m'darlin'."

Erin went cold with shock. "Amputated?" She stared at her grandmother. "What do you mean . . . amputated?" The word was repulsive and frightening.

Grandma looked at John. John looked at Erin. "Blue lost one of his front legs," he explained gently.

"No!" She could feel her face crumble.

"The vet had a choice," John said. "It was either that or let him bleed to death. We all wanted to save him."

The tears Erin had been holding back began to fall. She leaned against the wall for support. "No leg?" She shook her head in disbelief. "But he won't be able to walk or run or . . . or . . ." A sob stopped her. Blue wouldn't be going to the Campbell River Dog Show. Or any other dog show. Ever again.

He wasn't a champion anymore.

He wasn't perfect.

All because she had forgotten to use the springer.

Her mother reached for Erin's hand and gave it a squeeze.

She peered out through her tears. "That's . . . that's . . . that's horrible," she finally managed to say.

It was worse than horrible. As Cassie would say it was "majorly horrible". And it was all her fault.

"It is horrible," Grandma said with a slight smile. "But if Blue survives the next few days and makes it through physical therapy, he'll be all right. A little worse for the experience, but he should learn to walk again."

"But he'll have no quality of life," Erin said thickly. How *could* she have forgotten the harness? How *could* she have done it?

"He won't be a show dog anymore," John said. "But he'll still make a fine and loving pet."

Erin stared at him. Blue. Full of spunk and vinegar. The dog who couldn't wait to get up in the morning to chase birds or bring sticks. The dog who loved to chase butterflies and run beside her bike. The winner of this year's junior showmanship class.

The perfect Mr. Lavender Blue was perfect no more. All because she had been angry and upset and in too much of a hurry to get to Cassie's house. Erin couldn't choke back her sobs anymore.

"No!" Angry and ashamed, she turned from the kitchen and ran.

18

The back of the apple tree dug uncomfortably into her spine. Erin yawned and shifted her position slightly. She was tired; she hadn't been sleeping well since the accident four days ago. Blue had come through that first night and then the next. According to Dr. Maartens, he was going to be fine.

Erin wasn't sure she'd ever be fine again.

The late afternoon sun was hanging lower in the sky these days. The apples were starting to fall. Summer was almost over. In a few days, she would be going home.

Restlessly she tapped at a windfall apple with her toe. Once upon a time, Blue would have been there to chase it. Now the slightly lopsided piece of fruit rolled forward a bit and stopped. She could see a large black worm hole near the stem.

A worm. That's what she was. A worm.

Even if she didn't say a thing about the accident to Rachel, even if no one in school knew about Blue, she'd still be a worm. A stupid worm. And stupid worms didn't deserve to work at the SPCA.

She had made a mistake and it had cost Blue his leg. It had almost cost him his life.

A door slammed and she looked up. Her grandmother was heading slowly from the kennel run to the house, the feed bowl tucked casually under her arm. Was it her imagination, Erin wondered, or did her grandmother look older all of a sudden? Sadder maybe?

Grandma glanced to the right, saw Erin, and changed direction. "It'll be dinner time soon," she said when reached the tree. "Your mother's pot roast smells good."

Erin nodded. When her father had left to start his new job, Mom had stayed behind. Summer school was over. She said she deserved a little time off. Erin knew she had stayed behind because of Blue.

Slowly Grandma lowered herself to the ground. "Can I share your spot?" she asked.

Erin nodded a second time.

Her grandmother leaned back. "I want to tell you a story," she said, reaching for her hand.

"Okay."

"Once upon a time there was a girl, there was a dog, and there was a grandmother. The girl wanted to take her bike and the dog to the river. She asked her grand-mother for permission."

Erin swallowed the lump in her throat. Her grand-mother squeezed her hand and continued. "The grandmother knew all about leashes and harnesses and springers but the grandmother also knew about freedom. And so she said yes."

Erin's eyes filled with tears.

"There was an accident," Grandma continued gravely. "And the dog was hurt. Badly hurt. The girl felt terrible. So did the grandmother. The accident wouldn't have happened if a mistake hadn't been made. But mistakes are made and accidents happen. The girl and the grandmother learned from both. The dog recovered. He even learned to run again." Grandma smiled.

"But it was my fault!" Erin could feel the tears snake down her cheeks. "*My* fault," she repeated. "I didn't ask for your permission. And I rushed out of the house without thinking about the springer and the harness. You didn't make the mistake. I did."

Grandma pulled Erin into her arms. "But I could have m'darlin'. Easily. The truth is I never would have bought the springer. Never. It didn't occur to me until John showed up with it. I would have let you ride with Blue just like you did last year."

She wiped her tears away. "You're just saying that to make me feel better."

"No, I'm not!" Grandma pulled back and looked into Erin's eyes. Her gaze was steady, open. "Honest."

Erin frowned. "You said there was more traffic around here."

"Yes," the older woman agreed, "there is. But it's not something I think about every day. Now you listen to me, Erin Morris. What's over, is over. We have to move forward. I will not have you feeling guilty about what happened. Yes, you could have remembered the harness and springer. But the fact is, if it had been left up to me, you wouldn't have had that springer at all."

"Oh, Grandma." Erin began to sob. "I'm so sorry. I just wish it hadn't happened."

Grandma's arms went around her again. Soothingly she rubbed Erin's back. "I know what you wish, m'darlin'. But what's done is done. Don't look back. Look forward. Think of the future."

After a few minutes, her sobs turned to sniffles. Forward. Going home. Back to school. Leaving Blue.

Grandma pulled her up. "There's something I want you to do for me," she said, as they walked toward the house.

"What's that?" Erin asked.

"You haven't seen Blue since the accident. Your mom offered to take you a couple of times and you refused. I know it's a difficult thing to do, but I want you to go and see him. He's sad, Erin. Maybe you can cheer him up."

"Me?" She practically choked on the word. How could she do anything for Blue? She'd already ruined his life. There was nothing left to do.

"Yes," Grandma said, holding open the back door. "You. If you won't do it for me, do it for Blue."

* * * *

Erin could smell the animal hospital even before she walked through the door. It made her dizzy. Cassie gave her a good-natured shove forward. "Hurry up," she said. "Your grandma's waiting."

Grandma was ahead, speaking to a woman behind a tall white counter. Erin looked back over her shoulder, past Cassie, to her grandmother's car parked in the sun. If she could have her way she'd turn around, get into the car, and drive back to Dove Creek Kennels herself. Even though she couldn't drive. "This is a dumb idea," she whispered again to Cassie. "I don't want to be here."

"Your grandma wants you to." Cassie sat down on the edge of one of the hard wooden chairs. "Besides, like I told you on the phone last night, if you're going to work at the SPCA when you get home, you better get used to sick animals."

"You told me that this morning, too," Erin muttered crossly as she slid into the chair beside Cassie.

"It's true."

Erin glared at her. Sometimes Cassie's mouth was too big for her body. "You're supposed to be making me feel better, not worse!" She looked around the waiting room, at the dog magazines on the table and the pictures on the wall. There was a poster with an old English sheepdog. Its tongue was hanging out and it had a red ribbon around its neck. *Kiss me quick*, the caption read. A second picture showed a mother cat with a group of kittens curled up beside her. It reminded Erin of Duchess and her puppies.

It reminded her of Twister.

This was the place. The place they'd brought Twister to be put to sleep. The same day Blue had been hit by that car. The same day he'd lost his leg. She plugged her nose and tried not to breathe. "It stinks in here," she said to Cassie.

"You're just nervous," Cassie replied matter-of-factly.

"Shut up." With her fingers on her nose, the words came out in a squeak.

Cassie sniffed. "I'm going to pretend I didn't hear that," she said.

"Okay, girls." Grandma motioned them forward. "We can go in now."

Cassie stood. Panic seized Erin. She couldn't move. She didn't *want* to see Blue. She didn't *want* to see what she'd done to him. She shook her head no.

Cassie leaned close. "It's more scary thinking about it than doing it. My mom told me that and I hate to say it, but she's usually right." She pulled on Erin's elbow. "Come on," she said again.

Grandma gave her an encouraging smile. "Dr. Maartens is waiting for us."

It felt like forever before Erin could force her legs to work. Finally she stood.

The woman came out from behind the counter. She led them through a door and down a hallway. The horrible hospital disinfectant smell grew stronger. Erin's head felt like it was full of marshmallows. Her legs were wobbly like they got after she'd been sick for a very long time.

Click, click, click. The sound of their feet echoed off the walls. A dog barked in the distance; a man laughed. The woman stopped in front of a door that said "Recovery."

"Dr. Maartens is already with him," she told Grandma with a smile. She opened the door and Grandma stepped through.

Cassie looked at Erin. Erin looked at Cassie.

"Go," Cassie mouthed silently.

Erin swallowed the sour taste of fear that tickled the back of her throat. She went.

The recovery room was a long, skinny space like her grandmother's kennel. Running along one side was a series of cages — little rooms really — with metal bars that ran from floor to ceiling. On the other side were cupboards and a sink. Soft music played from an unseen radio. Slowly, slowly, Erin followed her grandmother past empty cages to one near the end.

"Hello, Dr. Maartens," Grandma said as she came to a stop. "How's Blue today?"

"About the same as yesterday," a voice replied. "Still a little too quiet for my liking."

Erin stopped suddenly and Cassie smashed into her back. Dr. Maartens was in the cage. So was Blue.

"Go," Cassie hissed.

She edged forward. Nervously she looked between the metal bars into the cage. Blue was asleep on his side. He had a large, white bandage wrapped around one haunch. Dr. Maartens was crouched beside him, a heavy-set man wearing khakis and a yellow sweater. She stared at Blue. For a minute she thought they'd

. a mistake. That he still had his other leg. But then she realized all that white was just a whole lot of bandage. With no leg inside. Her head felt all marshmallowy again. Quickly she looked away.

"Hello, Erin," Dr. Maartens said gently. His blue eyes were kind above his bushy gray moustache. "This must be very hard for you."

Tears gathered and stung. She opened her mouth to speak but she couldn't. The sour taste of fear was back and it was the size of a jawbreaker in her throat.

"She's very brave." Grandma gave her an encouraging smile.

Cassie jabbed her in the side. "Say something," she urged under her breath. "Talk to him. To Blue."

But Erin couldn't say a word. Dr. Maartens understood. "He's going to be fine, Erin," he assured her. "Even without his front leg. Blue's going to make it."

She nodded. Involuntarily her eyes were drawn back to Blue. The dog was stirring. "Hello, Blue," she whispered. "Hello, my darling Mr. Lavender Blue."

The dog sprang to life. He stood and tried to rush to the front of the cage. To Erin. With a whimper he crashed back to the ground. His tail thumped against the floor and he tried to pull himself forward, whimpering all the while.

Erin didn't know whether to laugh or cry. And so she did both. Dr. Maartens chuckled and stood up. "That's the most excitement I've seen out of him since he got here." He opened the door of the cage and motioned her inside. "Come on in," he said. "Somebody wants to say hi to you."

She hesitated. What if she touched his bandage? What if she hurt him all over again?

"It's okay." Dr. Maartens seemed to know what she was thinking. He shut the cage behind her. "Just kneel in front of him."

Erin tried. But before her knees touched the ground, Blue edged forward and lunged. He was all over her. His tongue was kissing her cheeks and her ears and her jaw, his nose was traveling back and forth across her face, through her hair, around her neck.

She steadied herself and threw her arms around him. "Hello, Blue, my Lavender Blue." She buried her face in his fur and let the tears fall again. "I'm so sorry, Blue. It's all my fault. I'm so sorry I —"

But Blue wouldn't let her finish. He began another enthusiastic round of kissing. He was still whimpering in excitement, his tail was still thump, thump, thumping madly against the floor.

"This is good to see." Dr. Maartens nodded approvingly. "Very good to see. Blue was improving physically but he hasn't been a very happy dog."

"Erin always was his favorite," Grandma said matter-of-factly. She and Cassie were watching Blue from outside the cage. "Even when he was a small puppy. I was hoping her visit would cheer him up."

"It certainly has." Dr. Maartens looked pleased.

But Erin's heart was breaking. With every kiss and every whimper she was reminded all over again of what she'd done to Blue. It was all her fault he'd lost

...ll her fault he'd never win another dog show.

"Blue needs a lot of love and attention," Dr. Maartens said when Blue was finally finished his kissing spree. "He's going to have to learn to walk and run all over again." The dog's head rested on Erin's knee; his eyes were dark and loving as they stared up at her. Every once in a while, when Erin looked back at him, his tail would thump against the floor.

God had answered her prayers, Erin reminded herself as she scratched Blue in that soft spot behind his ears. Half-answered them at least. Blue was okay. He hadn't died. But he wasn't full of spunk and vinegar like he used to be. And he never would be.

"It's going to take a special person," Dr. Maartens was saying. "Someone with a lot of time and patience to work with him."

"I think we can arrange that," Grandma said.

Something in her grandmother's voice made Erin look up. Grandma was smiling. Cassie was smiling. Dr. Maartens was smiling. "Pardon?" Erin frowned. She must have missed something.

"You wanted a dog, m'darlin'. And Blue's going to need a very special home. He's going to need what you were going to give to Twister. How about it, Erin?" Grandma raised her eyebrows. "How about taking Blue home with you?"

A three-legged dog? *Her* three-legged dog.

"No!" The answer was out of her mouth before she had time to think about it. "I . . . I . . . I can't do that." She jumped up. Blue whined at her sudden movement. "Come on, Cassie." She wouldn't look at

Dr. Maartens or her grandmother as she backed out of the cage. "Let's wait in the car."

* * * *

Erin played with her french fries, dipping them into the pool of vinegar on her plate and then into the little mound of salt. She'd been happy when her mother had suggested lunch at Mudsharks Coffee Bar, but after driving into downtown Courtenay and getting a seat on the terrace overlooking Fifth Street, her appetite had disappeared.

"You all packed?" Mom bit into a chicken wing.

Erin nodded. Dip, dip. Roll in salt. Dip again. "This summer has gone so fast." She sighed. Blue was home now, recuperating nicely, though he was still quiet at times, and not as energetic as Erin would have hoped. Dr. Maartens said to give him more time.

"It's nice that we've had some holiday time together."

Erin nodded a second time. Listlessly she bit into a French fry. Yuck. Too much salt.

"Don't eat it if you don't want to," Mom said. "This heat is enough to kill anyone's appetite."

"No kidding," Erin muttered. It wouldn't be so bad if she had worn shorts instead of pants this morning. But the hair on her legs was growing back just like Grandma had said it would. It felt like a thousand pins sticking out of her legs. And it looked just as ugly. She could shave. Mom would let her. She'd probably even let Erin henna her hair again, since the color was starting to fade. But it didn't seem to matter anymore. The perfect reinvention just wasn't the same without the perfect Mr. Lavender Blue to go with it. Erin pushed her plate away.

"I understand you have a decision to make," her mother said casually.

She knew exactly what her mother meant. "I've already made it."

Just then the waitress appeared with the bill. "Anything else for you?" she asked.

Mom smiled, shook her head, and handed the waitress a twenty-dollar bill. "Mistakes are funny things," her mother continued when the waitress was gone. "Most of the time you don't know you've made one until they're over but sometimes you can see them coming." She busied herself with the Caesar salad on her plate.

Erin frowned. "What do you mean?"

"Blue needs a home." She chewed her lettuce. "Grandma thinks he'd be happiest with you. Your dad and I think she's right."

She didn't answer. If she took Blue home, she'd be reminded every second of every day of the accident. Of her mistake. After that talk with her grandmother, she didn't feel guilty anymore. But she still felt responsible. After all, the accident was *her* fault. Nothing would change that.

"Here's a chance to right a wrong, Erin," her mother said in a soft voice. "To catch a mistake before it happens."

She watched a group of kids joke and giggle as they sat down at the table next to them. One of the girls had blonde hair just like Rachel. She knew what Rachel would say if she took Blue home.

Her mother followed Erin's eyes. "You're afraid of what the other kids will say, aren't you?"

She shrugged. "No. Yes. I don't know! You should see the way they treat this dog called Patches," she said. "It's awful."

"They could learn from you."

"Blue's just not the kind of dog I thought I'd get. He's . . . he's . . . he's just not."

Her mother's eyes were thoughtful. "Was Twister?" she asked.

"Twister was beautiful," Erin said hotly. "And he was a little puppy. Nobody makes fun of little puppies, besides, he had time to grow. Time to become perfect. And he would have been, too."

Mom smiled. "There's no such thing as perfection, sweetheart. We've all got our warts." Her eyes dropped to Erin's left hand. "Even if the real ones disappear, the imperfections are still there." She reached for another chicken wing. "Perfection isn't possible."

Her mother was wrong. "Yes, it is." Erin had tasted perfection. In the ring with Blue.

"People aren't perfect," her mother repeated as she licked her fingers. "Not Rachel, not me, not you, not your dad." She grinned and Erin could see a sliver of chicken stuck between her front teeth. "That's what makes us all so interesting. Same with dogs. They aren't perfect either. In fact, if you wait for the perfect dog to come along, you'll be waiting forever."

Guzzling her lemonade, Erin considered Mom's

words. Rachel not perfect? Or Mom or Dad, either? Okay, Rachel did have one eye that was bigger than the other, and she had a horrible temper sometimes. And Dad was impatient and Mom was obsessed with natural *everything*.

But what about the perfect reinvention? Well, even with all that work, Erin had to admit she was still clumsy and too tall and she daydreamed way too much. Not only that, if she was honest about it, the dog show hadn't been perfect either. Sure she and Blue had won. But she had tripped over that rock and Blue had almost refused to open his mouth and she'd practically missed that trick question about the breastbone.

If there wasn't any such thing as perfection, then what had she tasted in the ring? Maybe the purest form of happiness it was possible to taste.

"Think about taking Blue home," Mom suggested. "Okay?"

"Okay," Erin finally said. "But I'm not planning on changing my mind." A three-legged dog was worse than a bald and smelly one. She'd never live it down. And she'd never forget her mistake, either.

"Your dad and I love you, warts or no warts," her mother said, wiping her fingers on a napkin and pushing her plate away. "Don't you think Blue deserves the same thing?"

Epilogue

"I gotta go, Rach," Erin tried for the third time to get off the phone with her friend. She glanced at the red clock on the wall. Twenty minutes until Dan would be by to lock up for the night and she still had a lot to do.

"Then promise you'll come to the party with me?" Rachel giggled into the phone. "You gotta show off your cool new haircut and that great Gap sweater. Besides, the Oresti twins will be there and I think Zach Cameron will be, too," she added slyly.

Erin flushed at the mention of Zach's name. "I'll *see*," she said firmly. "Now I've got to go!" She hung up and turned back to the SPCA sponsor list on the desk in front of her. Same old Rachel. Still fixated on boys and clothes and looks.

She liked to look good, too, but right now she was more concerned with finishing the address list before she went home. Volunteering for the occasional night shift had its advantages. It was a lot quieter than working a weekend. She could get more done.

She began to write. A whimper from Blue stopped her. She looked up, her heart pounding the way it always did when Blue cried. The black Lab was sleeping in his favorite corner in the waiting room. His eyelids were twitching, his tail swished softly on the brown carpet. He whimpered again. Erin smiled. He was just dreaming.

Her heart slowed but she kept her eye on him. Unbelievable that she'd almost left him in Courtenay because she was so worried about what other people would think of a three-legged dog.

Zach Cameron seemed to think Blue was just fine. And, as far as boys went, Zach was fine, too. For one thing, he had a dog. A spunky Irish setter named Lucille. They sometimes bumped into each other walking their dogs on Grand Boulevard. Blue seemed to have a thing for redheads and Erin could tell Lucille had the hots for Blue. For another thing, Zach was taller than her, which meant she didn't have to look down when they talked, and he was gently playful with Blue, which she appreciated.

Erin returned to her list. The T's were done. No sponsors under U. Just a few under V and W and she'd be finished. If she kept taking on extra work and extra shifts, Dan was sure to give her a paying job. Erin really wanted a paying job. She could see it now.

She would buy a second Lab. A yellow this time. She'd call her Lilith or maybe Genevieve. Blue would be the dad and the new dog would have puppies. Lots and lots of puppies. Erin would go up and down Lonsdale putting up signs advertising the litter. Zach would help her. She wouldn't let the puppies go to just any -

"Excuse me."

Startled, she looked up. She hadn't heard the door open. Even Blue was still sleeping.

"Sorry if I scared you." A tall, silver-haired man gave her an apologetic smile. "I'm looking for my cat. He's been missing for three days."

Erin returned his smile. "Let me get the new arrivals list." She turned to the clipboard that hung on the wall behind her.

The door behind her flew open again. This time she heard it. So did Blue. He woke up with a woof.

"Here are your keys, Pops." There was a jingle of metal being tossed.

That voice. She would know it anywhere.

Clipboard in hand, she slowly turned around. Deryk Latham. Wearing his black leather jacket and standing beside the man who was obviously his father.

"H'lo," he said, meeting her eyes once and then quickly looking away. He shifted uncomfortably from one foot to the other.

Erin gave him one of those I-really-should-be-nice-so-I-will smiles. "Hello, Deryk," she said politely. He hadn't called her "Beast" once this year. The perfect reinvention had obviously changed his opinion about her. How silly. She was the very same person. Deryk was the same person, too. He still had that mean, spiteful look in his eyes, and he was still loud and annoying at school.

Blue hobbled over and nudged Deryk's hand. Deryk didn't look down but he did reach out to give him a scratch on the head. "We've lost our cat," he said, still moving uncomfortably on his feet.

"What does the cat look like?"

"Long-haired calico. Brown and white, with some orange," Mr. Latham responded. "Wears a bright green collar. Answers to Max. Has a chunk missing out of his right ear."

"We have raccoons near our place." Deryk's laugh sounded nervous. He ran a hand through his hair. "He probably got in a fight with one." Blue licked his hand. This time Deryk glanced down.

Did he see Blue's missing leg? She couldn't tell. "When did the cat disappear?" she asked.

"Halloween night," Mr. Latham said. "He hates loud noises."

She scanned back to October 31. Nothing. "I know we have a calico cat with a missing ear in one of the cages," she murmured out loud as she looked at the intake for November 1. "A male, too, I think. There he is. A brown and white long-haired." She read from Dan's notes. "Possible calico. Wearing a green collar. Looks well-cared for. Missing part of his right ear." Erin looked up and smiled. "Sounds like Max."

Mr. Latham looked relieved. Even Deryk smiled.

"Come on." She put the clipboard back on its hook. "I'll take you back to him." She walked out from

behind the desk. "Let's go, Blue." The black Lab hobbled to Erin's side.

Deryk's eyes widened. "That's Blue?" He stared at
the empty place where Blue's right front leg should
have been. "The champion you've been talking about?"

"That's him, all right." Erin pulled herself up and
looked Deryk Latham straight in the eye. "And he *is* a
champion." She grinned. "*My* champion. Now let's get
Max." She turned toward the kennel door.

"Woof!" Blue nudged her hand.

She laughed and gave him a playful tug on the ear.
"He doesn't like to be left behind," she explained to
Deryk and his father. She looked down into Blue's
warm, dark eyes. They held so much love . . . love she
had almost turned away from. "Okay, Blue," Erin said
softly. "Go ahead."

With his head up and tail held high, Mr. Lavender
Blue proudly led the way through the doors and back
to the cage that held Max the calico cat.

Acknowledgements

With thanks to Dr. John Ennals for his veterinary insight; to Chelsea, Lauren, and Judy Birmingham for their invaluable comments on dog shows; to agent Leona Trainer for a timely rescue; and to editor Lynne Missen for her sharp pencil.